The Brim Of His Hat And The Darkness Hid His Face From Her, And Somehow It Seemed Not As If He Was Looking At Her, But As If He Was Looking Through Her.

"You ever want to escape?" Alaina asked.

"Not at the moment."

His response made her pulse quicken. "That's not an answer."

D.J. leaned in, lowered his head so close she could feel his breath on her cheek. "I forget the question," he said.

So had she.

Dear Reader,

I can't resist a cowboy. A black Stetson, worn jeans and cowboy boots raise my pulse rate every time. If you remember Dylan Bradshaw from *Taming Blackhawk,* then you also might remember that this handsome, mysterious rancher was the ultimate lone wolf. (A big thank-you to all you readers who dropped me a line and asked me when I'd be writing his book!)

I've been wanting to tell D.J.'s story for a long time, but it wasn't easy to find the right woman for this reclusive, stubborn man. Until Alaina Blackhawk showed up. I knew, of course, that she was the perfect woman for D.J., but he was a little more difficult to convince. Not that D.J. didn't want the sweet, pretty Alaina in his bed—he most certainly did. But love and marriage? Not this confirmed bachelor!

Will Alaina's love and her "gift" be enough to heal the pain of D.J.'s past and tame his heart? You'll soon see....

Warm wishes,

Barbara McCauley

Visit me online at www.barbaramccauley.com to check out what's new!

BARBARA McCAULEY

BLACKHAWK'S BOND

Published by Silhouette Books

America's Publisher of Contemporary Romance

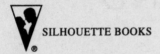

SILHOUETTE BOOKS

ISBN-13: 978-0-373-76766-3
ISBN-10:   0-373-76766-8

BLACKHAWK'S BOND

Visit Silhouette Books at www.eHarlequin.com

Printed in U.S.A.

Books in Barbara McCauley's SECRETS! series

Silhouette Desire

Blackhawk's Sweet Revenge #1230
Secret Baby Santos #1236
Killian's Passion #1242
Callan's Proposition #1290
Reese's Wild Wager #1360
Sinclair's Surprise Baby #1402
Taming Blackhawk #1437
In Blackhawk's Bed #1447
That Blackhawk Bride! #1491
Miss Pruitt's Private Life #1593
Blackhawk's Betrayal #1754
Blackhawk's Bond #1765

Intimate Moments

Gabriel's Honor #1024

Silhouette Books

Summer Gold
"A Wolf River Summer"

Blackhawk Legacy

BARBARA McCAULEY,

author of more than thirty novels for Silhouette Books, lives in Southern California with her own handsome hero husband, Frank, who makes it easy to believe in and write about the magic of romance. Barbara's stories have been nominated for and have won numerous awards, including the prestigious RITA® Award from the Romance Writers of America, Best Desire of the Year from *Romantic Times BOOKreviews* and Best Short Contemporary from National Reader's Choice Awards.

To Caroline Cross, for keeping me sane, and to
Jan Stockton, a real-life horsewoman and heroine.
Thanks for sharing your time, your knowledge
and your friendship.

One

The wolf paced.

Her wrists bound and staked firmly to the ground, she lay on her back and watched the animal tread back and forth, its large black paws moving smoothly and silently over the crisp leaves carpeting the forest floor. The scent of damp, fertile earth hung heavy in the still night air, filling her nostrils and lungs. Fear slithered up her spine and seeped into her blood. She opened her mouth to call out for help, but the words remained lodged in her throat.

Escape! her mind screamed at her, and she struggled to free herself from the thick ropes holding her arms above her head. Her limbs, heavy and leaden, refused to move.

Her pulse quickened, and she glanced back at the wolf. Its eyes glinting yellow, the animal paused and lifted its massive head, sniffed the air. A growl rumbled deep in its throat.

Dressed in ceremonial leathers, the Elders moved forth from the shadows of the trees that framed the inky sky. Their faces, tattered and worn, turned toward the wolf, and they nodded with solemn approval. A circle of fire burst forth, surrounding her, and the Elders vanished in the flames of brilliant red and gold. She called out to them, begged them to return, to set her free.

An eerie howl answered her.

She watched the wolf—no, a man—step through the flames. Her breath caught in her throat at the sight of his powerful warrior's body, naked, except for the loin-cloth slung low across his lean hips. Firelight danced in his long black hair, his sun-bronzed skin gleamed. Fierce, angry stripes of red and black war paint hid his face. Smoke clouded her vision, and the sound of distant drums beat in her head, through her rushing blood.

Panic swam through her when he approached, and once again she wrestled with the ropes at her wrist, but they held fast. He stood over her, gazed down with eyes the color of the sky.

"Submit to me," he demanded.

She shook her head.

He knelt beside her. "You belong to me."

"I belong to no man."

His smile flashed white through the haze of smoke. He slid his hand over her shoulder, down her arm. His palm was rough against her smooth skin. The ropes

*holding her, coarse and tight only a moment ago, turned
to velvet.*

She shivered at his touch.

"Submit to me," he repeated.

*"No." Her breath caught when his fingers loosened
the straps of the white sheath she wore. He peeled the
fabric back, baring her breasts. An arrow of heat shot
through her body; through her veins. Lightly he stroked
his fingertips down her throat.*

*Her chest rose and fell in short, air-gulping breaths.
Fear and anticipation consumed her. When he fisted his
hand and brushed his knuckles lightly over her breast,
the flames rose higher, hotter. He lowered his head, and
she felt the burn of his breath on her neck—*

Gasping for breath, her body shaking, Alaina Blackhawk bolted upright in bed. Eyes wide, she stared into the
darkness of her bedroom, then clasped a hand to her throat,
felt the pounding beat of her pulse against her fingers.

A dream, she told herself. *Just a dream.*

But it had felt so real, so incredibly real. She could
still smell the damp earth, the smoke. Could feel the bite
of the ropes on her wrists, the coarse texture of callused
hands skimming up her arms.

Her skin still tingled, her body throbbed with unful-
filled desire.

She hugged the bedclothes to her, waited for her
pulse to slow and the shivering to ease.

Pale streaks of moonlight slanted across the walls, into
the darkened corners. She drew in a deep, shuddering
breath, then dragged her trembling hands through her hair.

A sense of dread hovered over her like a great bird of prey, its large talons stretched wide, ready to swoop. She felt the breeze of its wings on her heated skin, looked up and realized it was her ceiling fan, nothing more.

She laughed dryly, then lay back down and pulled the sheets up to her chin. It was silly to be afraid of a dream. If anything, she told herself, she should have *enjoyed* it, even with all that "submit to me" nonsense.

The only thing she intended to submit to, she thought with determination, was a few more hours of sleep.

But even as her eyes closed and her skin cooled, even as she finally dozed off, she heard the distant sound of drums, and the lonely howl of a wolf....

No one looked twice at the dusty black pickup that turned off Highway 96 and headed east. This was Texas, after all. Trucks were as common in these parts as air, and there was nothing noteworthy about this one, anyway. No shiny paint job, no fancy rims, not one Don't Mess With Texas decal. When the pickup drove through the small town of Stone Ridge, the good folks simply nodded and gave a friendly wave, same as they would have done for anybody passing through.

But the driver of *this* truck, however, wasn't just "anybody," it was D. J. Bradshaw. *The D. J. Bradshaw.* And if folks had known *that,* jaws would have dropped faster than the Honorable Judge Pockerpine's oak-carved gavel.

It wasn't every day that the Lone Star state's most elusive—not to mention wealthiest—rancher showed his face in public.

And what a face it was.

D. J. Bradshaw personified the word *rugged.* With his large hands and powerful, six-foot-five frame, men said he'd been born to work the land he'd inherited from his daddy. Women, well, they thought those callused hands and muscled body had been born for something *much* more private.

And much more interesting.

Then there was that thick, devil-black hair and cobalt-blue eyes, that slash of dark brow and square-cut jaw, that hard set mouth and sun-bronzed skin. One look at D. J. Bradshaw and every woman—from the most refined female to the most demure maiden—was ready to slap on a cowboy hat and go for a ride.

Those lucky few who'd taken that ride still smiled at the mere mention of his name.

Once outside Stone Ridge town limits, D.J. slid a Bob Seger CD into the truck's player, cranked up "Against the Wind" then revved the engine and cut through the thick August heat rippling off the asphalt. No place better than a back country road to put pedal to metal, D.J. had always thought, taking the one-ton, 486 engine to full throttle. Gravel and dirt blasted off the back tires, leaving a generous layer of rubber on the road and dust in the heavy air.

"Bob" was singing about old-time rock and roll when the sign appeared twenty miles from the Louisiana border. D.J. slowed, then pulled off the main road onto a two mile, cedar-lined stretch of driveway leading to Stone Ridge Ranch. Golden ragwort splashed yellow across the lush green landscape, a sharp contrast to the prickly pear and rocky canyons he'd left only six hours ago.

D.J. drove under a tall iron archway with the SRR insignia, took note of the cattle and horses grazing beside a thick grove of fern-choked pines. When he rounded a grassy bend, a bridge stretched across a swiftly running stream and the truck tires clattered over the wooden planks.

He saw the stables first—red brick, with gray-shingled roof—and parked in front of them. He'd read a full report on Stone Ridge Stables weeks ago. Five thousand acres of prime timber and grazing land. Four ranch hands, one foreman, one housekeeper, a small herd of cattle and a stable full of prize winning quarter-horses. Though the ranch was legally owned by a woman named Helena Blackhawk, it was her son, Trey, and a daughter, Alaina, who ran the operation. There were two other daughters, as well. Alexis, who lived in New York, and the youngest, Kiera, who was a chef, and currently living in Wolf River.

D.J. liked to know the people he intended to do business with.

He'd also seen a detailed list of Stone Ridge Stables' profit and loss statements, bank accounts, a record of sellers and buyers they'd dealt with for the past five years. Information he'd need when he made the Black-hawks an offer to buy their ranch.

Stepping out of his truck, he caught sight of the main house and thought Southern antebellum. Thick vines of honeysuckle clamored up the white columns of the wraparound porch and a lush green lawn stretched across the front yard. To the west of the house, a stand of poplars shaded a rock and fern garden bordered with chunks of flat stone.

The scent of honeysuckle and the tinkling of wind chimes drifted on the hot, humid breeze, along with the amiable chatter of men working a horse from a nearby corral. He looked at his wristwatch, then glanced at the black underbelly of the clouds gathering on the horizon, hoped like hell he'd be back on the road before the storm blew in.

He started toward the house, stopped at the sound of a woman singing from inside the stables. He couldn't make out the words, but the melody was soft and sweet and vaguely familiar. It drew him into the stables, past several occupied stalls, until he came to the last open stall on the right.

Tall and slender, the woman stood with her back to him, brushing the muscular neck of a black stallion that had to be at least two hands above her head. Her hair, chestnut-brown, flowed in a thick ponytail down the back of her white sleeveless blouse. Her legs were long, her boots well worn. A bright red bandana peeked out from the back pocket of her snug faded jeans.

"Blue Bayou," he thought, recognizing the song.

He supposed he should say something. At the very least, clear his throat or shuffle a boot. Something to make her aware of his presence. But he was still curious, not to mention captivated by her voice and the slow caress of her delicate fingers sliding over the horse's sleek coat. The animal seemed captivated as well, D.J. noted. Except for a slight twitch in his left shoulder, the stallion stood motionless and calm.

When the woman stepped away from the horse and reached for a blanket hanging on a hook in the stall, D.J. allowed himself one last moment to appreciate her slender curves, then cleared his throat as he took a step forward.

Big mistake.

Startled, the stallion charged the open stall door. D.J. reached out and grabbed the lead line, but not in time to avoid the slash of a hoof across his forearm when the horse reared.

"Whoa!" D.J. held on when the horse reared up again. *"Whoa!"*

Nostrils flaring, black eyes wide, the horse dropped back down onto its front hooves, then jerked its massive head upward. The woman rushed forward and grabbed the animal's halter.

"Easy," she said firmly, then slid a hand down the stallion's neck. "Easy, boy."

Snorting, the horse pawed at the dirt and tossed its head. The woman grabbed the lead line and moved between D.J. and the animal. "I've got him now."

He let go of the line and stepped back, studied the woman's face as she led the horse back into the stall. Her features had an exotic appearance, but with a softer, smoother edge. High cheekbones, pale gold skin. A sweeping, narrow arch of dark brow over thickly lashed eyes as pale blue as an early morning sky. And her mouth. Damn. He let his gaze linger a moment on her upturned, lush, wide lips, and decided that his business here had suddenly become much more interesting.

"You're bleeding," she said.

He lifted his gaze to hers, saw the concern in her eyes. "What?"

"Your arm." She stepped away from the horse and glanced at him. "It's bleeding."

D.J. looked down. He'd been so distracted, he hadn't even noticed the gash on his arm or the blood dripping down his hand. *Damn.*

Her long legs closed the distance between them quickly. "Let me look at it."

"That's not—"

She reached for his arm. When he tried to shrug her off, she tightened her hold. "Be still," she said, using the same tone with him as she had with the horse. "It's deep."

Frowning, he watched her pull the bandana from her pocket and wrap it around his arm. When she applied pressure, he felt the warmth of her hand through the fabric. A tingling sensation, like tiny sparks of electricity, rippled over his skin, then shot up his arm.

What the hell?

Alaina Blackhawk glanced up sharply and met the man's narrowed gaze. Heart pounding, she stared at him, then jerked her hand from his arm.

"I'll get something to put on that," she said, backing away on knees that suddenly felt weak. "I, uh, have antiseptic, some bandages, in the tack room."

"Don't bother." Shaking his head, he removed the bandana. "It's barely a scratch."

Breath held, she looked down at his arm, saw that the bleeding had stopped and the cut was, indeed, barely more than a scratch.

It can't be.

Slowly, she lifted her gaze back to his. Even though heat still lingered in her fingertips, a chill shivered up her spine. "So it is," she said. "Just a scratch."

She heard the harsh, deep tone of his voice, knew that he had asked her something, but she was still too confused, her mind too muddled to understand. He'd tipped his black Stetson back and she could see his hair was the color of coal, his eyes a sharp, deep blue. A jagged scar ran beside the dark slash of his left eyebrow, and a bend at the bridge of his nose only added to the rough appeal of a man who clearly met life head-on.

She suddenly realized he'd asked her a question. "Excuse me?"

"I said—" he tilted his head, studied her "—are you all right?"

She fought her way through the cobwebs in her brain. "Yes, of course. You just startled me."

"Sorry." He looked at the stallion, watched the animal pace nervously in his stall, then glanced back at her. "I was looking for Trey Blackhawk."

She knew she should stop staring at him, that she should say or do *something*—at the very least, introduce herself. Even if she had practically been raised in a barn, she'd also been raised to be well-mannered, lest anyone think that the Blackhawk children were "heathens," so her mother had repeatedly said.

But she wasn't the only one staring. When his gaze swept down her neck, then her shoulders, and lingered for a moment on her breasts, Alaina's breath caught. She was twenty-seven years old, for God's sake. Men had looked at her before; for that matter, they'd looked a lot. It was only natural a woman who lived and worked predominantly with men was going to be stared at. But she'd gotten used to it, and most of the time, she didn't give it a thought.

This wasn't one of those times.

This time her body, with a will of its own, responded. Her pulse raced, her skin tingled, her breasts tightened. She watched his eyes darken, then slowly lift to meet hers. When he raised a questioning brow, it was all she could do not to turn and run.

"Alaina."

At the sound of Trey's voice, the force surrounding her vanished abruptly. Startled, she turned and saw him walking toward her. *Thank God.* She looked at her brother, his dark hair, his rock-hard features, that typical frown on his handsome face—and her world shifted back to normal.

Trey's gaze moved from his sister to the man standing a few feet away. "Mr. Bradshaw?"

"D.J." The man stepped forward to accept the hand Trey held out. "You must be Trey."

Bradshaw? Alaina watched the men shake hands. It took a moment to sink into her muddled brain, another moment to connect the dots. D.J., as in D. J. Bradshaw? The has-more-money-than-God, most-eligible-bachelor-in-Texas, D. J. Bradshaw?

"I see you've already met my sister," Trey said.

D.J. slid a glance in her direction. "Actually we hadn't gotten around to names. Alaina, is it?"

Because she couldn't risk touching him again—not just yet, anyway—she simply shoved her hands into her back pockets and nodded. "Mr. Bradshaw."

"D.J." He touched the brim of his hat.

"D.J.'s here to look at Santana," Trey said.

"Santana?" Alaina glanced at her brother. "Why?"

"There's been quite a buzz about the horse since you bought him from Charley Cooper last month." D.J. tipped his hat back. "Talk was two vets diagnosed him with navicular and he was going to be put down."

"Navicular is often misdiagnosed." It had been a stroke of good luck that she'd happen to hear about Santana and had managed to make a deal with the horse breeder. "Cooper should have gotten a third opinion."

"I agree." D.J. nodded. "Which is why my vet was out here two days ago."

Alaina narrowed her eyes in confusion. "Excuse me?"

"D.J.'s made an offer on Santana," Trey said. "Contingent on his own vet's report. You must have been in town when he stopped by."

Setting her teeth, she glanced back at her brother. "Yes, I must have been."

How convenient, she thought. Two days ago Trey had sent her into town to pick up a prescription for their mother. Somehow she managed to keep her tone casual. "Trey, could I have a word with you, please?"

Trey shook his head. "Later, Al."

"Now would be better."

"Alaina—"

"Go on ahead." D.J. slipped his thumbs into his belt and shrugged one broad shoulder. "I can wait."

"Thank you." Turning on her boot heels, Alaina walked out of the stables. A hot, northeast wind whipped up the loose strands of hair around her face and the oppressive humidity sucked the breath out of her lungs. If she had to commit murder, it was going to be a difficult day to drag the body out of sight.

When they were out of earshot, she whirled on her brother. "Why didn't you tell me?"

"About Bradshaw or Santana?"

"Dammit, Trey, don't patronize me," she said through gritted teeth. "You knew how I'd react."

"Exactly why I didn't tell you." Folding his arms, he stared down at her. "We're running a business here, Alaina. I haven't got time for this."

Alaina jammed her hands on her hips and met her brother's dismissive gaze. "You know perfectly well I'm still working with Santana."

"You told me his leg is healed." One of the ranch hands called to Trey, but he waved the man off. "If Bradshaw's vet agrees, then we've sold a horse. In case you've forgotten, Al, that's what we do here. Sell horses."

"In case you've forgotten—" frustration tightened her hands into fists "—I'm the one who makes sure our horses are ready to sell. And yes, his leg is healed, but I'm telling you he's still not ready."

"He's not ready?" Trey asked. "Or *you're* not ready?"

She opened her mouth to argue, then closed it again. "That's not fair, Trey."

"This isn't about fair." He wiped at the sweat beading his brow. "This is business. If Bradshaw wants the horse now, he gets the horse now."

"I just need a couple more weeks before—"

"If he makes an offer, it's a done deal." The distant rumble of thunder darkened Trey's frown. "So you and I can stand here and waste time locking horns about it, or you can accept it and move on."

"You're good at that, aren't you—moving on?" The sarcasm slipped out before she could stop it, and she bit her tongue, wished she could yank the words back.

A muscle jumped in his jaw. "Someone in this family has to be. We've got a ranch to run, Alaina. Bills don't get paid by sticking our heads in the clouds."

She sucked in a breath, let the sting of his words ripple through her. "Is that what you think I do around here? Stick my head in the clouds?"

Trey's mouth hardened, but he hadn't time to respond before another rumble of thunder sounded, louder and closer. They'd been so intent on their argument, neither one of them had noticed the dark clouds quickly sweeping in.

With a sigh, Trey lifted his hat and raked a hand through his hair. "No one works harder than you around here, sis," he said quietly. "And I know why Santana is special to you, but sometimes, even when you don't want to, you just gotta let it go."

Trey slipped his hat back on his head and walked away. Alaina opened her mouth to call him back, until she saw that D.J. stood just outside the stable entrance. Arms resting on the corral fence, he appeared to be watching two of the ranch hands saddle training a sorrel mare.

Horse breeders were a tight-knit community with loose tongues. When word got out—and it would—that Stone Ridge Stables had sold the stallion to Bradshaw, it would attract recognition and buyers from around the world.

D. J. Bradshaw had that kind of prestige and power.

And while none of that mattered to Alaina, she knew it mattered to Trey. And Trey mattered to her. No matter how much they argued and disagreed, no matter how many hurtful words might be said between them, she loved him.

Let it go, Trey had said.

Could she?

She watched him join Bradshaw at the corral and the men walked back into the stables. Closing her eyes, she drew in a slow breath, and knew she couldn't stop the sale of the horse any more than she could stop the rain that started to fall.

Two

The storm blew in fast and hard, bringing with it pitchforks of lightning and rolling claps of thunder. Rain fell in sheets, bounced off the dust dry dirt and formed pond-size puddles outside the stables. While ranch hands scurried about calming nervous horses and securing equipment, D.J. followed Trey up the wooden steps of the front porch.

"He's not easy to get in or out of a trailer." Stomping his boots on a thick door mat, Trey had to yell to be heard over the pounding rain. "If you decide to buy him, we'll deliver him to you."

D.J. shook the rain off and scraped the mud from his own boots, slipped off his hat when they stepped into the spacious front entry. The floors were glossy hardwood, and a fringed, burgundy and forest-green Oriental runner stretched toward a living room to the left. Walls the color of whipped butter displayed a collage of family photos that continued up a wide, oak paneled stairway and at the base of that stairway, a seven-foot mahogany grandfather clock loudly *tick-tocked,* drawing D.J.'s attention to the time. *Damn.* He'd hoped to be heading back home already.

A simultaneous bolt of lightning and slap of thunder struck close enough to make the house shake and the lights flicker.

"You might want to reconsider staying for dinner." Trey tossed his hat on a wall hook beside the front door. "At least wait for a break in the storm."

"Thanks." Though he was tempted by the tantalizing scent that filled the air, D.J. shook his head. "I'd like to get back on the road as soon as possible."

"You won't be gettin' nowhere tonight, not in this gully washer."

A man no taller—or wider—than a fence post came around the corner, wiping his hands on a green-striped kitchen towel. His eyebrows and moustache were as gray and wiry as the long hair he'd secured into a ponytail at the base of his skinny neck, and his eyes were nearly lost in a craggy sea of wrinkles.

"D.J., this is Cookie," Trey said with a wave of his hand. "Cookie, this is D. J. Bradshaw."

"Heard you was here." The elderly man skipped the dark slits of his eyes down D.J., then back up again. "You look like your pa."

D.J. noticed the old man's limp when he moved into the room. "You knew my father?"

"Can't say I knew him." Cookie shook his head. "Met him once, and your ma. She bought one of my apple pies at a county fair, more'n twenty years ago now. Said it was the best apple pie she'd ever had."

D.J. raised a brow. "Was that the Crowley County Fair?"

"That's the one." The elderly man shoved one corner of the towel into his belt buckle and held out a hand. "Won me a slew of blue ribbons that year."

"You were a celebrity in my house," D.J. said, shaking the man's hand. He'd only been thirteen at the time, but his mother hadn't stopped talking about that apple pie. "My mother told my father she was going to run away with you."

Cookie shrugged one bony shoulder and blushed. "Damn shame, what happened to your folks. A damn shame."

D.J. nodded. "Thanks."

Thunder grabbed hold of the house again and gave it another shake. Trey frowned at the flickering lights and looked at Cookie. "You were saying something about the storm when we walked in?"

"Big rig jackknifed out at the highway. Couldn't get out if you wanted," Cookie said. "Or git in. Jimmy called and said he was stuck ten cars deep and the sheriff is rerouting everyone back to town. Won't git a tow truck out till the morning, very least."

D.J. mentally echoed Trey's single swear word. Even

though he was obviously aware of the fact he couldn't do a damn thing about the situation, he still couldn't stop the knot of frustration tightening his gut. *So much for being home by midnight.*

"Was anyone hurt?"

D.J. glanced up at the dusky sound of the woman's voice and watched Alaina move down the stairs, couldn't stop the tug low in his belly. Her dark, thick braid hung over one shoulder of the red flannel shirt she'd changed into, and her jeans, a softer blue than she'd worn earlier, stretched across her slender hips and down her long legs.

"Hard to tell," Cookie replied. "Jimmy said three or four cars were smashed up and Drew Gibson's truck had flipped, but he was standing on the side of the road, kicking one of his tires, so I guess he's all right."

"Knowing that fool Drew, he probably caused the whole damn thing." Despite the sarcasm, there was concern in Trey's voice. "I'm going to call the sheriff and make sure Jimmy's not just looking for a night in town with Lucinda."

"I don't suppose you have another way out?" D.J. asked. "Maybe a back road?"

"Nothing that's even remotely passable in this weather." Trey shook his head. "Cookie set another place at the table, and Alaina, show D.J. to my office. I'll be right there."

D.J. watched Alaina open her mouth to protest, then quickly shut it again. Clearly she was not happy about having company. *That makes two of us, darlin',* he thought.

She led him down a wide hallway to a room rich with oak paneling and a wall of floor-to-ceiling glass that provided an ample view of the rolling hills surrounding the ranch. An impressive display of trophies, blue ribbons and silver buckles lined bookshelves, along with several framed certifications.

"I'm sure Trey won't be long." She gestured to a black leather armchair beside a large oak desk. "Have a seat, Mr. Bradshaw."

"D.J."

"Right." She turned and opened a leaded glass liquor cabinet. "What would you like?"

He slid his gaze down the smooth column of the woman's neck while he considered her question, decided it was best not to say the first thing that came to his mind. "Whiskey."

Might as well cut the edge off, he thought, watching the rain pour off the eaves outside the office. Even if the roads had been open, he knew he'd never make it home tonight in this kind of weather. With a little luck, that tow truck would get the highway cleared bright and early.

And based on the starch in Alaina Blackhawk's voice and shoulders, that was about as lucky as he'd get tonight.

"How's your arm?" she asked, opening a bottle of Jack Daniel's.

"Fine."

He came up behind her while she poured his drink, noticed the strands of hair that had escaped from the braid she'd knotted down her back. A strange urge to tuck them back into place took hold of him, but he resisted, and instead, leaned in and satisfied himself by drawing in the faint scent of jasmine drifting from her skin.

Her breath caught when she turned and found him standing so close. He had the distinct feeling she would have stepped away if her back hadn't been to the wall, but she recovered quickly and offered the glass to him.

"Thanks." When he took the glass, a spark snapped where their fingers touched. Raising a brow, he met her startled gaze.

"Static in the air," she said, her voice a bit breathless and snatched her hand away. "From the storm."

As if to punctuate her words, a flash of lightning illuminated the room, highlighted the red and gold in her dark hair and danced in her soft blue eyes. Her face seemed to glow and he had the urge to slide his fingers over her cheek, had to remind himself where he was and why he was here. Not to mention the woman's brother would be walking in at any moment. It didn't take a genius to figure out that making a pass at Alaina, as tempting as it was, wouldn't go over well with her brother.

Pity, he thought, then lifted his glass and sipped, enjoyed the spicy rip of flavor in his mouth. "You didn't come back to the barn."

"There was no reason to." She moved a shoulder. "Trey knows Santana. Once your vet comes back with a clean report—and he will—you'd have to be blind or stupid not to buy him. Obviously you're neither of those things."

"Careful, Alaina." He watched her over the rim of his glass. "That was almost a compliment."

Dropping her gaze, she turned to cap the bottle. "I apologize if I've been rude."

"I didn't say you were rude." He shifted his gaze to a far corner of the room. "But I am glad there's a lock on that gun cabinet over there."

When she turned back, there was a hint of a smile on her lips. "I know where the key is."

"I'll keep that in mind," he said, stepping back. "So you want to tell me why you don't want me to buy Santana?"

His question clearly caught her off guard and she turned, busied her hands adjusting bottles in the cabinet. "What makes you say that?"

"Like you said—" he sipped his drink "—I'm not blind or stupid."

She hesitated, then turned and met his gaze. "I'm still working with him."

"Trey told me." And obviously she wasn't ready to turn the job over to anyone else, he thought. It wasn't uncommon for trainers to be possessive and more than a little protective with their horses. "I assure you, my trainers are top-notch."

Thunder rumbled through the walls again, and a wind slashed rain against the windows. "I don't doubt that they are, but switching trainers, no matter how good they might be, can be difficult on some horses. Santana is used to me. He trusts me." Passion flared in her eyes, raced through her voice. "He knows that I—"

She bit her lip and glanced away.

Lord, don't stop now, he thought, fascinated by her swift and fervent outburst of emotion. "That you what?"

"Oh, Alaina, I'm sorry. I didn't realize you had company."

D.J. straightened and backed away, saw the woman standing in the doorway. An older, blond version of Alaina, he thought. Same pale blue eyes and face structure, same sweeping arch of brow. The linen blouse she wore was beige, her slacks brown. Her eyes darted nervously to the storm outside, then back again.

"Are you all right, Mom?" Alaina's voice softened. "Is something wrong?"

"I can't find Trey," Helena Blackhawk said, her words shaking slightly. "The storm—"

"Trey is fine." Alaina moved across the room. "He's just checking on the roads."

"Are you sure?" The woman placed a trembling hand to the rope of earth-tone beads at her throat. "He's been gone so long."

"He'll be right back." Alaina slipped an arm around her mother's shoulders. "This is D. J. Bradshaw. He's come to buy one of our horses."

"Mrs. Blackhawk." D.J. nodded at the woman. "A pleasure."

"Have you seen my son, Mr. Bradshaw?"

D.J. glanced at Alaina, saw the silent plea in her eyes, then glanced back at Helena and smiled. "Yes, ma'am. He was here just a minute ago."

"Oh, thank God." The woman sighed with relief. "My William died in a storm just like this one," she said. "Right after he saved a little boy from drowning. Did you know my husband, Mr. Bradshaw?"

"No, ma'am, but I am sorry for your—"

"Everything all right here?"

Trey stepped into the room and looked at Alaina, who nodded. "Mom was worried about you."

"I'm fine, Mom," Trey reassured his mother.

"You shouldn't be out in this storm." Helena reached out and touched her son's cheek, then glanced back at D.J. "No one should be. I'll have Cookie set another place at the table and prepare the guest room."

Rain fell steadily for the next few hours, and though an occasional rumble could be heard in the distance, the thunder and lightning had moved on. A typical summer storm, Alaina thought, standing at her bedroom window. She stared out into the black night, listened to the rain rushing through the gutters overhead. Weather like this blew in all the time.

What wasn't typical was what the weather had blown in with it.

She thought about the man sleeping in the guest room at the end of the hall, pressed a hand to her stomach and felt the flutter under the cotton nightshirt she wore. *So I'm not immune to D. J. Bradshaw's good looks and charm,* she thought irritably. A man who looked like that, with that kind of money and power, she'd have to be half-dead or in a coma not to respond, for crying out loud. It didn't mean a damn thing.

So then why can't you sleep?

Because of Santana, she told herself and turned away from the window. The horse had been stressed even before she'd brought him to the ranch, but the storm today had made him more tense. Knowing that he would be sold before she had the time she needed with the animal frustrated her, though not nearly as much as the fact that Trey hadn't even discussed the horse's sale with her, and that he'd intentionally sent her on an errand so she wouldn't find out. She knew that the ranch finances were strained because of their mother's medical and living expenses, just as she knew that those expenses were only going to increase over time. She'd tried to discuss the money situation with Trey, but he kept telling her that she needed to concern herself more with the horses and less with the money.

Lord, he made her want to spit nails.

Too keyed up to go to bed, she reached for her jeans and boots and pulled them on, then slipped into the hallway. The third step on the stairway creaked, as it always did, and at the same time she hit the last step, the grandfather clock started to bong out the midnight hour. Before it finished, she had her rain slicker on and was out the front door.

The aroma of Trey's Cuban cigars lingered on the front porch where, after dinner, he and D.J. had smoked. It was a scent she enjoyed, even though she thought it a nasty habit. Slipping the hood of her slicker over her head, she dashed across the yard to the stables, felt the pull of the mud under her boots every step of the way. In the distance to the north, silent lightning ripped through the sky and the energy of the storm exhilarated her.

With her mood lighter and her blood pumping, Alaina reached for the battery operated lantern hanging on a wall hook beside the stable doors. She flipped it on, filling the stables with a soft, golden glow. Pulling her slicker off, she threw it on a bale of hay, grabbed a fistful of oats, then made her way to Santana's stall.

"Hey, boy," she called to the stallion, who'd been pacing in his stall. The horse tossed his head and approached, then stretched his long neck and chomped on the oats she offered.

She stroked the animal's jaw while he ate, cleared her mind of the stress she'd been carrying all day. The smell of leather and hay and horse surrounded her and she closed her eyes, breathed the familiar scents in. The stables had always been her haven, a place where she could relax. There were so many memories here. Her first horse—a buckskin pony her mother had given her when she'd turned eight. The first time she'd seen a mare give birth. The first time Trey had let her help in the birthing.

There were other firsts, though with more mixed emotions. Her first kiss from Jeff Porter, a ranch hand's son. She'd been thirteen, in braces, and she'd had a painful crush on the lanky fourteen-year-old. The kiss had been sweet, but strangely disappointing. There had been other boys later, more kisses, equally disappointing.

"Must be me, huh, Santana?" Alaina smoothed her hand over the stallion's soft muzzle, frowned when the animal tossed its head. "Well, you needn't be rude," she said with annoyance. "So maybe I am different. Not much I can do about it."

Here in the stables was where she'd first learned just *how* different she was. Talk about mixed emotions.

"Can't sleep?"

She jumped back at the sound of D.J.'s voice, watched him move out of the shadows. "Good God," she snapped through clenched teeth and pressed a hand to her thumping heart. "You scared me."

"Sorry." Rain dripped from the brim of his hat. "I saw someone run out the front door to the stables and I thought there might be a problem."

"What do you mean, you saw me?"

"I was on the front porch."

He moved slowly into the circle of light surrounding her, approached her with the same caution one might use with a skittish horse. It amazed her how quietly such a large man could move. She suddenly felt awkward, and very much alone out here, two things she never felt in the stables.

She moved back to Santana's stall door, did her best to keep her tone matter-of-fact. "I thought you'd gone to bed."

"Going to bed and sleeping are two different things."

Her cheeks warmed at his comment, though she was certain he hadn't intended anything suggestive. At least, she didn't *think* he did. She glanced at him, watched him casually lean one broad shoulder against the stall frame and decided it was simply her own awareness of the man that made her think about sex.

She put her hand out for Santana, and the stallion snorted softly against her palm. "I hope there wasn't a problem with the accommodations."

"The accommodations—" he repeated the formal word with amusement in his voice "—were excellent, as was the dinner and the company. I appreciate the hospitality, especially considering the fact you and your family were stuck with me."

"I'd say it was the other way around." She doubted very many people—especially women—would consider themselves "stuck" with D. J. Bradshaw. "And my mother enjoys company, especially when she's staying at the ranch."

"She doesn't live here?"

"Not for the past couple of years. Her doctor in Austin thought—" Alaina hesitated, had no idea why she was discussing her mother's state of health with a complete stranger. "It's just better for her to be in the city, so she only comes out to the ranch for short visits. We don't have very many guests here, other than an occasional friend one of my sisters might bring home."

"Alexis and Kiera."

It surprised her that he knew their names, but then she remembered her mother had talked about them during dinner. Thankfully her mother had done most of the talking, telling story after story that may or may not have happened. But if D.J. had been uncomfortable with Helena Blackhawk's obvious obsession with the past, he hadn't shown it. He'd been a perfect gentleman and listened attentively, said all the right things at all the right times.

Which is what he seemed to be doing now, she thought and decided there was a very fine line between manipulation and control.

"When my sisters were in college they always thought it was funny to bring their city pals to the ranch and give them a taste of the country life. We used to place bets on how long the different friends would last." Alaina smiled at the memory. "After a couple of days without their lattes and sushi, most of those friends were chomping frantically at the bit to escape from here."

"And you?" D.J. reached out a hand to Santana, but the horse tossed his head and backed away. "Were you ever chomping at the bit to escape?"

"Me?" She laughed at the idea, remembered her one trip to New York and how overwhelmed she'd felt. All the cars packed in, the horns honking, the herds of people. She hadn't been able to breathe. "No, I missed my sisters, and I understood their decisions to leave here, but the ranch was my life. Is my life. Simple as that."

"Something tells me there's not one thing about you that's simple," D.J. said quietly.

The brim of his hat and the darkness hid his face from her, and somehow it seemed not as if he was looking at her, but as if he was looking *through* her. The thought sent shivers up her spine. She felt the heat of his body, smelled the masculine scent of his skin, knew if she touched his chin, the dark stubble of his beard would vibrate through her fingertips. Her awareness of him, of his closeness, made her wary and more than a little anxious.

"What about you?" Somehow, she managed to keep

her voice conversational. "You ever want to escape? Be someone or someplace other than where you are?"

"Not at the moment."

His response made her pulse quicken. This time, there was no question there was a suggestive tone in his voice. "That's not an answer."

He leaned in, lowered his head close enough she could feel his breath on her cheek. "I forgot the question," he said.

So had she.

She knew she should tell him to back off, or back away herself, but she seemed incapable of either. The rain drummed softly on the roof and the darkness closed in, heightened her already overloaded senses, until she swore she could hear the beat of his heart and taste the passion.

Smell the danger.

His mouth was within an inch of hers, then closer. Anticipation shivered through her and she waited, breath held, but didn't move.

Neither did he.

Frustrated, she nearly closed the whisper of space between their lips, until she realized that was exactly what he wanted her to do. *Not gonna happen, Bradshaw,* she thought and eased back.

He watched her for a moment, then slowly raised a brow. "You're not curious?"

His question rippled over her like a warm wave. *Hell, yes.* But she'd be damned if she'd let him know that.

"I'm curious about D. J. Bradshaw," she said, managing to find a thread of calm and hold onto it.

"Curious why a man with your kind of money and status took up so much of his valuable time to drive so far and look at one horse."

"I'm a hands-on kind of guy."

She imagined that was quite an understatement, and the image of those hands on her made her take a step back. "Or maybe you're just bored and looking for a little diversion."

"If I was just bored and looking for a diversion," he said with a slow smile, "I assure you, I wouldn't need to drive eight hours."

Whether they were talking about horses or women, if D. J. Bradshaw wanted either one, Alaina had no doubt that he wouldn't have to move even one of those big, strong muscles of his. All he'd have to do was crook one finger.

"No, I don't suppose you would." Turning, she reached for the lamp. "I should be getting back in."

"My vet called about an hour ago."

Her hand jerked, then closed around the handle and she turned back. "Oh?"

"He gave Santana a clean bill of health." He paused a moment, as if to measure her response, then said, "His leg is good as new."

She'd known what the vet's report would be, and even though she'd had all evening to prepare herself, she still couldn't stop the sharp little slice of pain in her heart. She hated that Trey was right, that she'd become too emotionally attached.

How could she not?

"Congratulations," she said, though the word felt hollow. "You've bought yourself a magnificent horse."

"Actually—" D.J. straightened "—I haven't made my decision yet."

"I don't understand." She furrowed her brow. "Trey said your decision was based on the vet's report."

"It was. Now it's based on you."

"Me?"

"I'd still like to buy Santana," he said, "but only if you'll come along and finish his training at the Rocking B."

"What?" Certain she hadn't heard him right, she simply stared.

"You said you needed more time with the horse, so I'm offering it to you."

"At your ranch?"

"At my ranch."

"You're kidding, right?" She locked her knees into place so they wouldn't buckle on her. "Why would you do that?"

"Several reasons." Tipping his hat back, he folded his arms. "One, like you said earlier, changing trainers could result in a setback."

"Still—"

"Two," he went on. "I have a brood mare arriving in two weeks and I think she's perfect for Santana. I need the stallion ready for her, or we'll miss her season. And worst case scenario, we lose control during the breeding and Santana reinjuries his back leg."

Alaina was well aware of the fact that when a stallion covered a mare, there were always potential problems and injuries, to both horses. The breeding process needed to be kept as controlled as possible.

"Three, I'd like to watch you."

Her spine stiffened and she lifted a chin. "Excuse me?"

"Watch you work." He emphasized the last word. "I'm impressed with your style."

"My style?" Now she *knew* he was kidding. "You know nothing about me."

"I know what I see. It's obvious you've had phenomenal success with Santana in a short period of time. I've seen you with him, how he responds to you. I'm not so shortsighted not to realize there's always something to be learned, Alaina."

She raised the lamp and looked into his eyes, but was unable to read his expression. "What did Trey say about this?"

"I figured I should talk to you first." D.J. met her gaze straight-on. "But I understand if you'd rather discuss it with him before you give me an answer."

Alaina knew perfectly well what Trey would say if she took this deal to him. It didn't matter that she was twenty-seven years old and more than capable of taking care of herself, Trey's overly protective side would have instantly said no. And if D.J. hadn't asked her first, Alaina had no doubt that Trey would never have even told her. He simply would have said that the deal had fallen through.

And D.J. knew it, too.

She'd spent her entire life sheltered, stayed within the safety net of family and the ranch. While Alexis and

Kiera had fought for their freedom and won it, Alaina had chosen to let Trey make all the decisions in her life, business and personal. It had been easier that way.

Safer.

But now, suddenly, she had an opportunity to make a decision for herself, for the ranch, and though the thought of it turned her stomach inside out, it also thrilled her. She would not only have the extra time she so badly needed with Santana, but an opportunity to actually work on one of the largest and most famous horse ranches in the entire state of Texas.

How could she say no?

She stared at D.J., considered the possibility he might have a fourth reason for her to come work at his ranch, but then she dismissed the idea. He'd been toying with her tonight, playing head games, but D. J. Bradshaw was a businessman. His decision would have been based solely on facts, not a frivolous, passing moment between two strangers. She doubted that a man like D.J. would give the moment, or her, a second thought.

She stared at D.J., knew he was giving her time to think, but she also knew he wanted an answer now. In the quiet of the barn, she was certain he could hear the hammering of her heart.

Two weeks, at the Rocking B with D.J. As much as the man unsettled her, surely she could handle two weeks.

She ran through several scenarios as to how she might approach Trey on the subject. Calm and logical was the first one. Determined and steadfast was the second. Angry and in his face was the third. But no matter how they started, they all ended the same. He'd yell, then forbid it, then they'd fight about it and he'd yell some more. She'd never won an argument with her brother, not over something as big as this, and she had no reason to think this time was going to be any different.

But for her, this time was different. This time it really mattered. This time it was something *she* wanted.

So the question was, did she want to do this the hard way, or the easy way?

It didn't take two seconds to come up with an answer to *that* question.

Drawing in a slow breath, she straightened her shoulders and met D.J.'s dark gaze. "All right," she said and nodded slowly. "I'll do it. But on one condition…"

Three

"So you're telling me that Trey Blackhawk doesn't know?"

D.J. looked over his shoulder at Judd Mitchell, his ranch foreman. They'd just ridden in from looking over the yearlings in the north pasture and had one of their weekly "business meetings," which covered everything from animals to equipment to staff. There wasn't anything that happened on the Rocking B that Judd didn't know about, and more than one ranch hand had grumbled that the man must have eyes in the back of his head.

D.J. had considered not telling his foreman about the arrangement he'd made with Alaina two days ago, but decided the man would figure it out anyway. And since she was expected to arrive within the hour, D.J. figured now was better than later.

"That's the way she wanted it." D.J.'s horse, a roan gelding named Sergeant's Duty, blazed his way through a thick patch of devil's grass. "No skin off my nose."

"Might be," Judd said.

The edge of accusation in Judd's tone had D.J. pulling up the reins on his horse. "What's that supposed to mean?"

Judd reined Roxie, his dapple gray, next to Sergeant. "Means he might take exception to you failing to mention that you made a side deal with his sister."

D.J. shrugged, knew that whether he wanted it or not, there was advice coming. "She offered up the terms, I accepted."

When Judd snorted, D.J. lifted a brow and met his foreman's steady brown gaze. At forty-six, Judd had a face that resembled the bark of a pine tree, and a long, straight, solid body that looked like the trunk. He was the only man on the Rocking B who D.J. would tolerate giving him a lecture, and even with Judd, there were limits.

"She might have set the terms." Judd glanced overhead at the soft blue, late afternoon sky, watched a Cooper's hawk glide, then dive into a grove of cypress. "But you set her up."

"What the hell is that supposed to mean?"

"She didn't have to come here to finish the horse's training." There was no judgment in Judd's statement, only question. "She could have worked at her own place for the next two weeks, then delivered the stallion in time for breeding."

"Santana's high strung," D.J. said, his irritation mounting. Sergeant, sensing his rider's mood, stomped a hoof and flicked his tail. "The horse is used to her, and I want the transition to go smooth."

Judd's saddle creaked when he pushed up the brim of his white hat and leaned back. "You talking about the transition of the horse, or the transition of you buying Stone Ridge Stables?"

"I haven't even made an offer yet."

"But you will."

He already had a lawyer drawing up the paper-work. "I will."

"Don't expect she'd take kindly to you withholding that little piece of information," Judd said dryly.

"Don't expect she will."

Judd nodded, let the silence pass between them for a moment. "So is she pretty?"

"What the hell difference does that make?" D.J. snapped. "I'm running a business here, dammit. Her looks have nothing to do with my decision."

The amusement in Judd's eyes had D.J. clenching his jaw. His foreman had gone fishing and D.J., idiot that he was, had just swallowed the bait whole.

"She's good with horses," D.J. said flatly. "The men might learn something watching her work."

"You want her working with the men?"

"That's her decision." But D.J. thought about a few of the younger, randy men whose brains weren't in their heads, but located much farther south. "You just make sure no one steps out of line."

Judd smiled slowly. "You included?"

D.J.'s reply comment was short and rude and when he nudged Sergeant into a trot, Judd's laughter followed.

Alaina turned off the highway and drove another thirty miles into a pretty valley with rolling hills and large outcroppings of rock. The summer heat had browned the mesquite and low growing shrubs, but groves of cypress and oaks stood tall alongside a slow moving river. This was Rocking B land, as far as the eye could see and way beyond. Acre after acre, mile after mile of picturesque land in the Texas sun belt. Late afternoon sun glistened off the water and glowed in the treetops, dappled the pastures and meadows.

When she passed the first outbuilding and paddock, her hands tightened around the steering wheel and she drew in a slow breath. It wasn't the first time today she'd questioned her sanity. She doubted it would be her last.

You're a grown woman, she told herself. *You have a right to make your own choices.*

Still, the deception—or omission of truth—depending on how she looked at it, did not sit well with her. Guilt was a useless emotion, as tough to shake as a burr on wool. But she'd made her decision, shook hands on the agreement and she wouldn't back down now.

The knot of nerves in her stomach tightened as she passed more paddocks and outbuildings, and when she rounded a bend and spotted the main house, her jaw went slack. She'd seen large ranch houses before, had delivered more than one horse to wealthy clients who lived in

mansion-size homes. But this was something else alto-
gether and Alaina eased up on the gas pedal to gawk.

The two-story house towered upward from the surrounding oak trees, a blend of split granite stone and
river rock with a diversity of peaked roof lines, stone
chimneys and leaded paned windows. The structure
blended well with the landscaping, a stark use of native
shrubs and grasses and rock.

She decided the house fit the man. Solid, big and
more than a little foreboding.

As if her thought had conjured him up, she saw him
then, dismounting a roan by one of the corrals. Two big
dogs, one black, one gold, danced at his heels. His back
was to her, but she recognized the black Stetson and
those broad shoulders. He'd rolled the sleeves of his
white shirt to his elbows, and his faded jeans rode low
on his lean hips.

When he turned at the sound of her truck and lifted
his gaze to hers, her heart jumped. Once again she questioned the sanity of her coming here, then once again
thought about the horse in the trailer behind her.

Slowing the truck to a crawl, she watched a young,
sandy-haired man run over to D.J. and take the reins of
his mount. When D.J. glanced over his shoulder at
another man riding up on a dapple gray and spoke to
him, she resisted the urge to look in the mirror and
straighten the hair she'd clipped on top of her head,
settled for a quick hand comb to sweep back the loose
strands. *As if it matters,* she thought, annoyed at her
feminine impulse to primp for a good-looking man. She

was wearing a faded pink T-shirt, old jeans and cowboy boots, for crying out loud. Not exactly the kind of outfit that gave a man ideas.

And not that she *wanted* to give him any ideas, either. She didn't. She just wanted to look presentable, that's all.

She pulled in front of the barn and watched him walk toward the truck, his long strides slow and easy. She placed a hand over her stomach when it started to tap dance, then flipped her air conditioner on high to cool the heat on her cheeks.

She rolled her window down when he reached the truck door. "This okay here?"

"Fine." He reached for the door and opened it. "Leave the keys in it. One of the men will move it later."

Nodding, she cut the engine and slid out of the truck, wished she could stretch the kinks out of her shoulders and legs, but decided against it. Based on the curious stares coming from the men working in the corrals, she thought it best not to draw any more attention to herself than necessary.

But then she looked back at D.J., felt the heat of his gaze slide over her, her throat turned dry as the dirt under her boots.

And then suddenly the dogs were racing across the yard toward her, barking a friendly and excited greeting. Alaina braced herself for the incoming missiles and the impending impact.

"Baxter! Taffy!" D.J. yelled at the dogs, who just managed to stop short of launching themselves. "Sit!"

The animals braked to a halt mere inches from her and sat, their bodies quivering with tightly coiled energy.

"Any problems?" D.J. asked.

"Hit a little traffic in Houston." She rubbed a hand over the black dog's head, then the gold one. Tongues rolling, they both pressed against her palm for more. "Smooth sailing from there on."

"Any other problems?"

"If you mean my brother, he wasn't too fond of me delivering Santana by myself." To say that Trey had been adamantly opposed was an understatement. They'd argued about it for twelve hours straight yesterday. Well, actually, *she'd* argued. He just kept saying no and walking away. "He wanted to come with me."

"And you convinced him otherwise," D.J. said, stating the obvious.

"I told him that I need some time off and since the Rocking B is practically on the way, I'm going to visit my sister when I leave here."

"The sister in Wolf River?" D.J. tilted his hat back. "Kiera, right?"

"Yes, Kiera." The man had a hell of a memory, Alaina thought, and reached into the cab of her truck for her leather gloves. "I doubt he would have bought it if I'd told him I was driving to New York."

"I suppose not," he replied with a grin. "So are you?"

D.J.'s smile stirred up the butterflies in her stomach. "Am I what?"

"Going to see your sister?"

"Well, of course I am," she said, with a touch of indignance. "I wouldn't lie to my brother. I just didn't give him a time frame between my leaving here and going there."

"I see." D.J. lifted a brow.

"He was still going to come with me." She'd had to think fast when Trey had made that announcement. "Until I told him that Kiera and I were going to be planning her upcoming wedding. He backed off so fast, he nearly tripped over himself."

She'd watched her brother face angry bulls and growling bears, but the only time she'd seen the man flinch was at the mention of marriage. She looked at D.J., could have sworn he'd leaned back himself when she'd mentioned the "w" word.

Men, she thought, shaking her head.

"Long as I call or leave him a text message every couple of days, he won't bother me." *Or you,* she thought, pulling her gloves on. "You've got me for two weeks, Mr. Bradshaw," she said and gestured to the trailer. "Let's go take a look at your horse, shall we?"

It took an hour before Alaina managed to persuade the anxious stallion out of the trailer. Several of the hands had circled in as well. A couple had offered to help—obviously hoping to make a good impression on the pretty woman—and Alaina had politely allowed them to try. One of the men had hobbled off in embarrassment after a hoof made contact with his knee, and another bowlegged cowboy had slunk back after the horse had managed to nip him hard enough on the arm to draw blood.

With Judd at his shoulder, D.J. had stood back and

quietly watched, decided to let the men see for them-selves that Alaina knew what she was doing. When she finally coaxed the animal out of the trailer, without bodily harm to her or the horse, the men clapped.

"Show's over," D.J. barked when the men hovered. "Bobby, show Miss Blackhawk to Santana's stall. I'll be there in a minute."

Bobby, a baby-faced kid from Montana with curly blond hair, tripped over his feet, then blushed when Alaina smiled at him. D.J. rolled his eyes when they walked away with Santana.

"Good choice," Judd commented. "Pair her up with the youngest, shyest pup. Especially her being so homely and all."

"I'm not pairing her up with anyone." The hands had slowly strolled back to the corrals, but not without casting furtive glances over their shoulders at Alaina and mumbling to each other. "And I never said she was homely."

"Never said she wasn't, neither."

D.J. frowned at his foreman. "You wanna sharpen whatever point it is you're trying to make?"

"Production's gonna seriously drop with a woman around," he said simply and shrugged. "Especially one who looks like that."

D.J. watched Alaina lead Santana into the barn, couldn't stop his eyes from drifting down and watching the sway of feminine hips. Judd had a point, dammit, D.J. realized. If he couldn't keep his eyes and thoughts under control, how the hell did he expect his men to?

Only one way, he figured.

"Tell them she's with me," D.J. said tightly.

Judd lifted one bushy brow. "You sure about that?"

Hell, yes, he was sure. He didn't want his hands standing around drooling over a woman when there was work to be done. What they did on their own time was their business. But then he realized he didn't want them drooling over Alaina on their own time, either.

"Just imply it." He looked over at the men, saw them grinning at each other and laughing, figured they were already taking bets on who would score with the pretty brunette first. The thought settled in his gut like a shard of green glass. "That ought to keep them out of trouble."

"Sounds like it's going to get you *into* trouble." Judd pushed his hat back and cocked his head. "Somehow, I don't think Alaina's going to appreciate your effort to protect her virtue."

"She's only here for two weeks," D.J said with a shrug. "It's for her own good."

"Whatever you say, boss."

"Just remember that." D.J. frowned as his foreman then headed for the barn where Bobby, was busily pitching fresh straw into Santana's stall while Alaina filled a trough with water. The stallion flattened his ears and jerked his head back when D.J. leaned against the stall door.

D.J. frowned at the horse. "I'm beginning to take this personal."

Smiling, Alaina closed the spigot, then reached out to stroke the stallion's nose. "He just needs a little time to adjust. Don't you, boy?"

The horse snorted, then tossed his head, as if to say no, which made Bobby laugh. When D.J. turned his frown on the ranch hand, he sobered up and put his back into pitching more straw.

"You must be tired after your drive," D.J. said. "Bobby can take care of things here."

"I'm fine." She led the horse to the trough and put her hand in the water, enticing the horse to drink. "I'm sure Bobby has other things to do."

"No, ma'am," Bobby said, eager to please. "I can feed him and brush him, too, if he'll let me."

Alaina glanced at Santana, and D.J. wasn't sure if she hesitated because she didn't want to leave the horse, or she was nervous about going with him.

"I don't mind, really," Bobby added. "You go on."

Got to give that kid a raise, D.J. thought when Alaina reluctantly nodded. She quietly murmured something to the horse and smoothed a hand down its neck. "Just a handful of oats and some hay, and if you really want to make friends, he's a sucker for a slice of apple."

"I'll find one," Bobby said with such enthusiasm that D.J. knew he'd drive all the way to town and buy one if he couldn't. Hell, he'd probably drive to the next county, D.J. thought, and wondered if he'd made a mistake choosing Bobby to help Alaina. She'd barely been here an hour and the boy was already smitten. In two weeks, he'd be a complete goner. Poor kid was about to get his heart broke and he didn't even know it.

Alaina handed the lead line to Bobby, then wiped her hands on the front of her jeans. "All right, then," she said, glancing over. "I'll just get my bag out of the truck."

"I think I can manage that." D.J. opened the stall door for her and closed it after she passed through. "Dottie sees you carry your own suitcase and I'll be in a world of hurt."

"Dottie?"

"My housekeeper." They walked to the truck and D.J. plucked the suitcase from the back seat of the crew cab. "She's been jumping out of her skin since she heard you were coming. We don't get much female company and she's looking forward to having another woman in the house."

Alaina's heart stumbled at D.J.'s words. *His house?* She hesitated, watched him stride ahead of her. "I'm staying in your house?"

D.J.'s boots clunked across the slate stone walkway. "Of course. Where did you think you would stay?"

"Well, I—I don't know. I guess I just assumed I'd be in the bunkhouse."

D.J. paused, narrowed a look at her over his shoulder. "With the men?"

She glanced at the ranch hands, saw a couple of them watching her. No, she supposed that wasn't a good idea. But then she looked back at D.J. and didn't think sleeping in his house was such a good idea, either. She considered getting a room in town, but then she'd not only be on the road a couple hours a day back and forth, she wouldn't be close to Santana.

The lesser of two evils? she wondered, then hurried after D.J. when he continued on toward the house.

She caught up with him as he was reaching for the front doorknob

"What will your men think?" she asked.

D.J. stilled, then looked down at her and frowned. "I don't give a damn what my men think."

She realized she was acting like a child. She was an adult, a grown woman, not the odd, shy little girl who'd endured the giggles in school and the whispers in town. What did it matter what his ranch hands—or *anyone*, for that matter—thought about her? She'd spent too much of life worrying about that sort of thing. No more, she told herself.

But before she could respond, the front door flew open.

"You're here! Oh, come in, come in! I'm Dottie."

She was a short woman, big-boned, with tightly trimmed silver hair that swept back from her face like the fins of a 1955 Falcon. Glittering green eyes nearly disappeared beneath the deep lines of her smile and matched the color of her short-sleeved blouse.

"I saw your truck drive up over an hour ago and been waitin' on pins and needles." Still pumping Alaina's hand, Dottie looked at D.J. and clucked her tongue. "Shame on you, Dillan Joseph, making this poor girl work her first day here."

Alaina glanced at D.J., who gave her an I-told-you-so-look.

"I am here to work," Alaina said, overwhelmed and amused at the same time and wondering when the woman was going to let go of her hand.

"Not your first day, you're not." Dottie pulled her into

the house. "I made my special roast for supper and a dessert that makes a grown man reach for a hankie."

D.J.'s eyes lit up as he closed the door. "You made chocolate cake?"

"Don't you be sneaking a piece." Dottie finally let go of Alaina's hand and shook a finger at D.J. "And don't think I won't know if you stick a finger in the frosting, either."

At the sound of a buzzer from the other room, Dottie swung around. "That's my potato casserole," she said, then shot D.J. a look. "I'm sure Alaina wants to freshen up before dinner. You show her to her room and I'll get her something wet and cold."

"Please don't go to any trouble on my account," Alaina said, but the woman had already hurried off.

"There's no stopping her when she's like this." D.J. moved toward a sweeping staircase. "Best thing to do is just ride it out. She'll calm down in a few days."

A few days? Alaina turned to follow D.J., then stopped in her tracks. If it wasn't enough that Dottie had been overwhelming, D.J.'s house was simply staggering. Cathedral ceilings that had to be over twenty feet high. Hardwood floors so smooth you could slide in your socks from one room to the next, windows so tall a giraffe could see in. And though it was a masculine house, the layers of bright rugs, pine moldings and antique furniture softened the harsh edges.

"This is beautiful." Wanting to take it all in, she looked up and turned slowly, watched the rays of the late afternoon sun stream in through an overhead skylight.

A smile on her face, she glanced at D.J. He stood on the stairs, watching her and when her gaze met his, her pulse leaped. The look in his eyes, hungry and intense, made her breath catch.

"Land sakes, what are you still doing here?" A glass of lemonade in her hand, Dottie came back into the entry. "You sure didn't get very far."

"I was just admiring the house," Alaina said, struggling to compose herself.

"Mr. B built it for D.J.'s mama. Such a shame they never got to live here." Dottie shook her head and sighed, then frowned at the sound of a muffled meow. "That fool cat. She had kittens three weeks ago and she won't stay put with them. Keeps moving them all over the house."

"Keep her out of my bedroom," D.J. grumbled.

"Esmeralda—that's the cat—" Dottie lowered her voice "—she moved her babies to his bed for a couple of days and poor D.J. slept on the sofa till she moved them again. He'll deny it if you ask him, though. Says he doesn't like cats."

"Dammit, Dottie, I told you I just fell asleep on the sofa, that's all," D.J. barked and started back up the stairs. "And I *don't* like cats."

Dottie's grin said she knew better and she handed the glass of lemonade to Alaina. "Here you go, honey, this should take the dust out of your throat. I best go see where Essie has moved her family to this time."

"Thank you." Alaina watched the woman disappear around a corner, then she looked back at D.J., who'd nearly reached the landing. She took a long gulp of the lemonade and followed after him, certain that the ice-cold drink, or even ten ice-cold drinks, wouldn't be enough to wash away the dryness in her throat.

Four

The last time that the dining room in D.J.'s house had seen a guest was three years ago, when Dottie's sister, June, had visited the ranch. Dottie had gone through the same rigmarole then as she had tonight. The china came out of the cabinet, the silver had been polished, the cloth napkins ironed. And in the center of the eight-foot-long table, a crystal vase filled with flowers cut fresh from her garden just that morning.

D.J. thought it was silly for three people to eat at a table that seated twelve, especially when the kitchen table was smaller and more comfortable than the formal setting of the dining room. But he knew women liked the hubbub of entertaining, so he figured he could manage to indulge Dottie's overblown display of social pleasantries for at least one night.

Not that he really had a choice. He might own the place, but everyone knew who the real boss in this house was.

"My Velma's first baby, Bridget Ann, she popped out like a piece of toast," Dottie was telling Alaina. "But the next one, little Timmy, he hung on tight as a tick, till they finally did a C-section. Velma swore no more children after that, but now here she is, eight months pregnant and looks like she's ready to pop."

Oh, for God's sake. D.J.'s fingers tightened on the fork in his hand. It was one thing to sit through Dottie's endless tales of her own three grown children, but stories about childbirth and babies popping out was just going too far.

D.J. pushed his plate away and cleared his throat.

Dottie didn't pause. Instead she moved on to the next daughter, Marlene, and her first pregnancy. And since Marlene had four kids, D.J. knew that this line of conversation was going to take a while.

He cleared his throat again, a little louder this time, and Dottie glanced over at him.

"Coffee?" he asked.

"We'd love some," Dottie said, but when D.J. frowned, she lifted her brow and rose from her chair. "Oh, right. All this carrying on when I've got cake in the kitchen. Silly me. I'll be right back."

Alaina reached for her plate and started to rise. "I'll help."

"Absolutely not." Dottie snatched the plate from her

and flapped a hand in protest. "Don't you dare move a muscle. You're a guest in this house."

"Thank you, but—"

"No buts." Dottie shook her head. "I insist."

Alaina looked at D.J., as if imploring him to change the woman's mind, but he simply shrugged.

"Now, I have coffee, regular or decaf," Dottie offered while she collected silverware and plates. "Or maybe you'd like some tea? I have peppermint, orange pekoe or Earl Grey. Then, of course, there's milk, whole or skim, or a bottle of brandy that's just screaming to be opened."

"Coffee is fine," Alaina answered, her eyes a bit wide. "Regular, please. Black."

When Dottie scurried away, D.J. watched Alaina shift in her chair. The meal had been easy while Dottie was there, chattering away like a squirrel with a bag of acorns. But now it was just the two of them and Alaina was clearly uncomfortable. She folded her napkin, folded it again.

"I'm sorry for any inconvenience I've caused," she said when she finally looked up. "I'm sure you have better things to do than sit here and listen to all this woman talk."

During the meal, D.J. had thought of at least a dozen things he'd rather be doing. Mucking out stalls, scrubbing down troughs. Jumping off a cliff. But at the moment, he couldn't think of anything but the way Alaina had looked this afternoon when she'd stood under that shaft of light streaming down through the entry skylight. Shades of red and gold had danced in her thick, dark hair and her entire body had seemed to glow silver-white. The smile on her wide lips and pleasure in her soft blue eyes had felt like a fist to his gut.

He'd taken a long shower after he'd showed Alaina to her room. A cold one.

"I'm just here for the cake." He sat back in his chair. "And trust me, Dottie is having a great time."

"The way she cooks, I'm surprised you aren't bigger." Her cheeks turned pink and she bit her lip. "I mean, that you're in such good shape."

Her cheeks turned even pinker.

"Thanks." He grinned at her. "You're in pretty good shape yourself."

He hadn't seen a woman blush in a long time, and it looked damn pretty, he decided. She mumbled a thank you, then fiddled with her napkin again. He watched her long, slender fingers sliding over the fabric, smoothing and folding. He remembered what her hands had felt like the first time she'd touched him in her barn. And though the sensation had been extraordinary, it had also been invigorating somehow and he hadn't been able to get it out of his. Hadn't been able to stop wondering what her hands would feel like moving over more than his arm.

The thought sent an arrow of heat straight to his groin and he decided they needed to talk about something other than what kind of shape they were both in.

"I know a Blackhawk," D.J. said casually and stretched his legs out under the table.

Alaina's hands stilled on the napkin. "It's a common name."

"Rand Blackhawk." Based on the stiffness in her shoulders and voice, he'd obviously pushed a button. "He was a horse trainer just outside of San Antonio, but he's got a ranch in Wolf River now. Didn't you say your sister lives there?"

"She's only been there a month." Alaina reached for her water glass. "She's a chef at the Four Winds Hotel. Have you heard of it?"

He had the distinct feeling she was trying to change the subject, which only made him more curious. "That's quite a coincidence," he said as he watched her take a long sip of water. "Rand's sister, Clair, owns the Four Winds."

"I've never met them."

Again, an answer that wasn't an answer. If the Blackhawks in Wolf River were related to Alaina, she clearly preferred not to say so. He hadn't talked to Rand since he'd gotten married a few months ago. D.J. considered giving his friend a call, maybe ask a couple of questions.

Alaina rose from her chair. "I should see if Dottie needs any help in the—"

"There we are, now." Dottie bounded in from the kitchen carrying a wooden tray loaded with mugs of coffee, giant wedges of chocolate cake and a glass bowl of whipped cream. She set the tray on the table, then scooped a fluffy cloud of cream on each slice. Smiling, she placed a plate in front of Alaina, then D.J. "I've turned down three marriage proposals after serving this."

"I was one of them," D.J. said and dug into his slice, was savoring that first delicious taste of chocolate when he made the mistake of looking at Alaina. He watched her take a delicate bite, then slowly slide the fork out of her mouth. A look of sheer pleasure lit her soft blue eyes just before she closed them and moaned softly.

Damn if his heart didn't thump against his rib cage.

While she heaped praise on Dottie, D.J. slouched his shoulders and hunkered down over his plate, careful not to look at Alaina again. He'd be damned if he'd let a woman interfere with his appetite.

"It's all in the chocolate," Dottie explained to Alaina. "I have to order it special from this little town in—oh, Esmerelda! There you are."

D.J. glanced over and saw the black and white cat sitting in the dining room doorway, looking as if she owned the whole damn world. She'd always been a barn cat, but somehow she'd managed to slip into the house to have her kittens and Dottie adamantly refused to put her back outside until they were older.

He *didn't* like cats, blast it. Only thing they were good for was mousing, he figured, and since the animal had moved into the house, she wasn't even good for that. She'd not only taken over his bedroom for two days with those kittens of hers, but to add insult to injury, the ungrateful feline barely gave him the time of day.

At the moment, Queen Esmeralda was staring with interest at Alaina.

"Aren't you a pretty lady?" Alaina said sweetly and held out her hand.

The cat stood and stretched, as if to say, "Yes, aren't

I?" then strolled slowly over and rubbed her head against Alaina's fingers. D.J. could hear the cat purring all the way across the table.

He watched Alaina stroke her hand over Esmeralda's arched back, and there it was again. The need to feel her touching him. Frowning, he stood, tossed his napkin on the table and grabbed his coffee.

"I've got work in my office," he said and looked at Alaina. "You need anything, just ask Dottie."

The dream found her, reeled her into the forest mists and laid her gently on a bed of soft leaves. The stillness soothed her and she breathed in the quiet, then sighed with contentment. She belonged here, in this place where the spirit of her ancestors shimmered on the cool night air. From the thick shadows, she felt their eyes on her, watching...waiting.

The wolf howled.

A sudden wind whipped through the trees and she shivered at the icy chill that snaked through her veins. She tried to stand, to run, but her arms and legs were so heavy. A bolt of fire shot upward from the ground, then another, and another, until a circle of crackling flames surrounded her. A ribbon of smoke curled toward her, wrapped around her wrists and bound them together. She struggled, but could not break free.

She watched the man emerge from the flames, and she fought to stay calm. She'd known he would come, had waited for him. He was The One.

But the wavering shadows and smoke hid his face

and uncertain, she shrank back. What if she was wrong? Would she lose her power?

He moved closer to her, all sinewy muscle and glistening skin. The chill in her blood heated, spread through her body. I am weak, she thought, biting her lip against the throbbing need. So weak.

He lowered his body, moved over her, slid his hands up her arms to her bound wrists.

"Submit to me," he whispered, his voice husky.

If only she could see his face. If only she could touch him, as he touched her. Then they would both know the truth. When his mouth dropped to her neck and nipped, she trembled. No! she thought. I can't—

Alaina bolted upright in bed. *Where am I?* Frightened, she glanced around the strange room, for a moment thought she was still dreaming, then the haze cleared from her brain and she remembered where she was.

D.J.'s house.

The air she'd sucked into her lungs shuddered out. *That dream!* she thought, clutching the soft cotton sheets to her breasts. *That damn dream!* It was bad enough she'd had it in her own bed three nights ago, but now it had followed her here, to the Rocking B. Her heart was still clamoring in her chest when she dropped back onto the bed.

"It doesn't mean anything," she whispered and curled up tightly. "It *doesn't*."

Like a mantra, she repeated the words over and over, until she almost believed them. Alaina flipped from her side to her back, stared at the ceiling for a full two minutes, tapped her fingertips together for another minute, then flipped to her other side.

After the long day of driving, then the huge meal that Dottie had prepared, she should have slept like a baby all night. Instead—she glanced at the bedside clock— she was lying here wide-awake at 4:00 a.m.

Still, Alaina reasoned, she was in a strange bed, a strange house. It was understandable that she was a little tense. She flipped to her back again. Okay, so she was a *lot* tense. That was understandable, too.

She was sleeping in D. J. Bradshaw's house, for heaven's sake. Or, at least, *trying* to sleep, she thought with a sigh. Dottie had given her a tour of the house after dinner, and she knew that his bedroom was at the end of the hall. She could still see his king-size bed clearly in her mind. The massive oak headboard, the Navajo print bedspread, a pair of black boots dropped casually on the hardwood floor at the foot of the bed.

It had all felt so…intimate.

At least with another woman in the house, Alaina wasn't quite so tense. She knew Dottie was downstairs, in the bedroom off the living room, and the thought comforted her. The housekeeper would be the buffer that Alaina needed between herself and D.J. She wouldn't deny that the man made her nervous. And it wasn't just D.J. she didn't trust, either.

It was herself.

He made her think things, made her feel things, she'd never thought or felt before. And though she might be naïve when it came to the opposite sex, she wasn't so completely inexperienced not to recognize that look in a man's eye. D.J. had made it clear he was attracted to her, and there was no doubt in her mind that he knew she was attracted to him, as well. If they'd been alone here in this house for two weeks, there was no telling what might have happened.

Bless you, Dottie.

As long as the woman was under the same roof with them, Alaina was certain she had nothing to worry about.

Stop acting like a child and go to sleep, she told herself sharply, then closed her eyes. She listened to the quiet, heard the house settling around her, the slow, deep sound of her breathing…and then the faint, steady beat of a drum…

Her eyes popped open again and she swore, threw the covers off, then got up and dressed.

Five

It was his favorite time of the morning. Just before
the sun skimmed the horizon and turned the sky pale
gray, just before the men clomped out of the bunk-
houses, slurping coffee and jangling spurs. The air
was cool and still, heavy with the scent of dew. If you
listened carefully, very carefully, you could hear...
nothing.

Dropping his hat onto his head, he made his way
toward the barn, paused at the end of the walkway and
glanced back at the second-story bedroom window
where Alaina, like the rest of the ranch, was sleeping.

An image crept into his head, the same image he'd
kicked out of his mind probably a hundred times last
night. Those long legs of hers stretched out on her bed,

her dark hair fanned out around her pillow, her lips softly parted with sleep,

A hell of an image.

Females were a distraction on the ranch, especially females who looked like Alaina. It was the main reason he'd never brought any of the women he'd dated to the Rocking B. Not only because women got ideas when you brought them home, but because he preferred to keep work and women separate.

Alaina was the first woman who had fallen into both categories. He'd asked her here for business reasons, but he desired her physically, as well. An interesting dilemma. He hadn't decided yet if he would just let nature take its course and see what happened, or if he'd give it a nudge. Either way, he thought a nice long ride out across his valley to check on the water pumps in the south pasture would not only cool his blood, but give his mind time to clear. Dottie wouldn't have breakfast on the table for two hours, anyway. Might as well get a jump on the day.

He was halfway across the yard when the sound of boots and the clunk of hooves on hard dirt pulled him up short. Narrowing his eyes, he watched Alaina walk out of the darkness, leading Santana behind her. He blinked to make sure she wasn't an illusion he'd conjured up by simply thinking about her.

"Mornin'," she greeted him and moved closer, her braid draped over the shoulder of her denim jacket.

Her voice had a throaty, still half-asleep tone, and the sound was like warm silk sliding over his skin. She was real all right. "You're up early."

"Thought I'd take Santana for a walk around the corrals before things got busy around here, let him get used to the smells and feel of the place without any distractions." She reached up and patted the horse's neck, then glanced back. "You're up pretty early yourself."

"I've got some pumps to check out in one of the pastures." He held his hand out to the horse and the stallion tossed his head up, but didn't back away. "Why don't you ride along, get the lay of the land? I'll show you some trails you can take Santana on when he's ready."

"I don't know." She looked at the dark house. "I told Dottie I'd see her—"

"Dottie won't be up for an hour and she puts breakfast out an hour after that." When she still hesitated, he started toward the stables. "Come on, I'll saddle up Gypsy Belle for you. We'll be back before the food hits the table."

"Gypsy Belle?" Alaina hurried after him. "Isn't she the mare that won the national futurity last year?"

He thought that might get her attention. "Yep."

"And you'd let me ride her?"

"Sure." He flipped the light on in the barn, watched a few sleepy horses stick their heads over their stall doors. "If you want to."

"If I *want* to?" Her eyes lit up like it was Christmas morning. "You're kidding, right?"

"Nope." He opened Gypsy's stall door, and the pretty chestnut mare nuzzled his shirt pocket, hoping for a treat. "She's a little spirited. Think you can handle her?"

"Gosh, I don't know." She shook her head as if she doubted herself, but there was a smile in her eyes. "I'm just a girl."

Hardly, he thought and grinned. "I'll saddle her up while you put Santana away."

"D.J."

He'd already started to open Gypsy's stall when she called his name. He glanced over his shoulder, saw the uncertainty on her face. "Yeah?"

"Last night—" She hesitated, then drew in a breath. "Last night you asked me about Rand Blackhawk."

"Just making conversation." The smile had disappeared from her eyes, and he realized he missed it.

"If I'm going to be here for two weeks," she said firmly. "I'd just like to say it now and get it out of the way."

Folding his arms, he leaned back against the stall door, watched the play of emotions move across her face and the tight press of her lips. Whatever it was she wanted to say, it obviously wasn't easy.

"Rand is my cousin, my father's nephew." She stared into one of the dark stalls, drew in a breath and met his gaze. "You've probably heard of William Blackhawk. He owned the Circle B in Wolf River."

"William Blackhawk is your father?" Of course D.J. had heard of him. He'd never actually had any dealings with the man, but the Circle B was one of the largest cattle ranches in the state.

"I don't really remember him," she continued. "I was only five when he left."

D.J. remembered what Helena Blackhawk had said

about her husband drowning, realized the pieces weren't quite fitting together. "He left?"

Absently Alaina stroked Santana's neck. "I know what my mother told you, and she truly does believe that's what happened to my father. We don't know where she came up with the story, but over the years she's convinced herself, her children, even the people in Stone Ridge, that her husband had died trying to save a little boy who'd fallen into a river. It was easier than accepting the fact that she'd had a ten-year affair with a married man, then been paid off when he was done with her and his illegitimate children."

An affair. Now it was beginning to make sense. D.J. bit back the swear word on the tip of his tongue. While he'd thought there might be a connection between Alaina's family and the Blackhawks in Wolf River, he'd certainly never considered it would be quite so close.

"Alaina," he said quietly, "you don't have to tell me any of this."

"I know I don't have to, but if you know Rand, you'd hear this sooner or later, and I'd just as soon you heard it from me." She used her fingers to comb back the loose strands of hair falling across her cheeks. "Trey and Alexis and I have all known the truth about our father for years—we even knew three years ago when he was killed in a plane crash."

D.J. realized she hadn't mentioned the youngest sister. "And Kiera?"

Alaina shook her head. "We kept the truth from her. She's our baby sister and we all thought we were protecting her. A few weeks ago, Alexis and I decided it was time for her to know, but Trey wanted to wait until she got settled into a chef's position she'd accepted in Europe. She overheard us arguing about it, then went to Wolf River herself, without telling us. She can be very impulsive."

D.J. lifted a brow and grinned at her. "Like you coming here?"

"That was practical," she insisted, but there was a smile in her eyes. "Anyway, when Trey found out, he went there to rescue her, so he thought. But it turned out she didn't want, or need, to be rescued. She's engaged now, to the manager of the Four Winds, and is building a relationship with our father's family, including Rand, and his wife, Grace."

D.J. had been at Rand and Grace's wedding a few months back, had never seen two people more in love, or happy. "They're good people."

"Yes," she said softly, glanced down at the lead line in her hand and sighed. "Did Rand ever tell you he was adopted?"

D.J. shook his head. "He worked here as a trainer for me a few years back and we stayed friends after he left, but we never talked much about family."

Santana gave an impatient snort and Alaina laid a hand on the horse's cheek to calm him. "His parents were killed in a car accident when he was a little boy. He was in the car, too, but he survived, along with his brother, Seth, and his sister, Clair."

Alaina paused, as if she needed to compose herself,

then met D.J.'s eyes. "My father was the only living relative, and when he was called to the scene of the accident, he separated the children, then paid a man, a lawyer, to adopt them out, letting Rand and Seth think their siblings had died. Clair, whose birth name was Elizabeth, was too little to remember."

It took D.J. a moment to wrap his brain around the enormity of Alaina's words. William Blackhawk had sold off his orphaned nephews and niece? Not even knowing what the hell to say, he just shook his head on one simple, earthy swear word.

"They've all found each other again," Alaina said, and there was relief in her voice. "I'll be meeting them for the first time when I leave here. But knowing what my father did to them…"

She dropped her gaze, but not before he saw the shame there. "Like I said—" D.J. pushed away from the stall "—they're good people, smart enough to know you aren't your father."

Nodding, she drew in a deep breath and lifted her eyes. "Thank you."

"No thanks necessary." He tamped down the unexpected need to touch her, to comfort, and instead, shrugged one shoulder and turned to open Gypsy's stall door. "Now how 'bout we take that ride?"

They rode south across the valley, through a thick grove of cypress and dogwoods. Along the eastern skyline, a silent trumpet of pale blue blared across the horizon, while in the branches overhead, birds greeted the new day with loud chirps and fluttering wings. The air was cool, heavy with the scent of wild sage and peppergrass, and somewhere to the left of her, though she couldn't see it, Alaina could hear the sound of tumbling water.

Gypsy Belle pranced under her, and Alaina knew that the chestnut mare wanted to take the lead, rather than follow. And while she might respect the horse for that, Alaina was perfectly happy to keep her distance behind D.J. Not only because he knew the way, but because it gave her an opportunity to study the man without him knowing it.

He looked good in the saddle, she thought. He sat tall, his broad shoulders completely at ease, his long legs the right fit for the large roan gelding he sat astride. Of course, since she'd been raised on a ranch, she'd seen a lot of men who looked good in the saddle. Some who'd even looked better than good.

But never one who made her mouth water.

When he glanced back at her, she quickly looked away, pretended to be studying the trail. It was bad enough she'd snatched at the carrot he'd dangled by offering to let her ride Gypsy Belle, the last thing she wanted was for him to know she was staring at him, too.

She'd surprised herself by dragging her family skeletons out of the closet. She'd carefully guarded those demons, had kept them under lock and key in a basement of shame and disgrace. But for some reason, she couldn't bear the thought of D.J. hearing about her father and the horrible things he'd done from anyone else. She'd needed to tell him for herself. Needed to see his eyes. Needed to know if he would look at her differently, treat her differently.

He hadn't. He simply listened, without judgment, without turning away, and for the first time in her life, if only a little, her shame had lightened.

"Up here," he said, and pulled her out of her thoughts. She glanced in the direction he pointed, toward a narrow path leading upward through a patch of boulders and brush. Though it seemed odd to be riding uphill when they were headed for a pasture, Alaina gave Gypsy Belle her head, knowing the horse could see much better in the dim light than she could.

The trail turned steeper and narrower, and they picked their way through a rock and dirt trail edged with prickly pear and shrubs of mesquite. She watched a rabbit peek out from a bush, its nose twitching anxiously, and she prepared herself, just in case that cute little bunny or one of his friends decided to dart across the trail. They continued upward, maybe for another thirty yards or so, until the trail widened and finally leveled out to a large, flat summit.

They were on a mesa, she realized and followed D.J. to a large oak. "I thought you were going to check on the pasture pumps."

"We will." He dismounted and walked over to her. "I want to show you something."

Suspicious, she glanced around, suddenly felt way too alone. "Graves of all the other women you've enticed up here?"

He laughed softly. "You're the first."

She wasn't sure if that was a comforting statement or not, but she could just make out his face in the gray light and saw the amusement shine in his eyes.

"Hurry up. We haven't got much time."

"Time for what?" she asked, watched him turn and walk away. He didn't reply, just gestured for her to follow. She bit her lip and looked around. She was on an isolated mesa, and absolutely no one in the world—other than D.J.—knew where she was. Call her crazy, but she was just a little nervous.

Or maybe excited.

"Hurry," he called back to her.

"What do you think, girl?" Alaina patted Gypsy Belle's neck. "Should I follow him?"

The animal pawed the ground and snorted. Not much of an answer, Alaina thought with a frown, then drew in a deep breath and dismounted.

He stood on the edge of the mesa, his back to her, and she moved closer. The air was cooler up here, lighter, the only sound a rustling of the leaves through the low brush.

Inching her way toward him, she was no more than a few feet away when he lifted an arm and pointed at the horizon. "There."

She turned her eyes to the skyline, watched the first brilliant slit of sun emerge from the rugged hilltops. Silver-white, the rays streamed upward, transforming the dull gray sky to baby-blue. Below them the valley, bisected by a river, stretched out like a carpet of soft browns and pretty greens. Specks of cattle and horses dotted the pasture and hillsides, and windmills, at least ten that she could see, towered above the landscape, swirling in the dawn's breeze.

Awestruck, she watched the sunrise, could feel the beauty of it shimmering through her.

"Pretty, isn't it?" D.J. said and turned to look at Alaina. He'd brought her here on an impulse, and seeing the wonder and amazement on her face, he was glad that he had.

"Beautiful," she murmured.

He moved beside her, pointed to a stand of tall cypress. "There's an eagle living in those trees, and if you look close, on the other side of the river, that's where the deer gather to drink."

She squinted, then whispered breathlessly, "Oh, I see them. There's so many."

He watched her gaze dance over the valley, taking it all in, couldn't help the swell of pride in his chest.

"I don't know how my sister does it," she said softly.

"Kiera?"

She shook her head. "Alexis. It amazes me that we're identical twins."

D.J. tried to picture Alaina's twin, but couldn't imagine another woman who looked like the one standing in front of him. "You don't know how she does what?"

"Lives in New York." Alaina looked back at him. "All that concrete and steel blocking out the sun. Noisy, crowded streets, jammed with people rushing about. Why would anybody choose to live like that?"

He'd wondered that himself, especially on the days

he'd come up here. "Guess that what makes life interesting. Different people, different choices."

She scanned the valley again, and drew in a sharp breath. "Oh, look, the eagle!"

D.J. watched the bird lift out of the trees and soar across the sunrise. When he looked back at Alaina, he saw the moisture in her eyes and frowned. "You okay?"

"I think I'm just a little overwhelmed by it all." Laughing, she wiped at her eyes with the back of her hands. "Sorry."

"Don't be." He pulled her hands from her face, and with his thumb, wiped away a tear sliding down her cheek.

And then it was there again, he thought. That… feeling. It was nothing he could exactly put his finger on, sort of a vibration he sensed whenever he touched her. Or whenever she touched him. Something stirred inside him and he looked down at her, watched the sunrise bloom over her face and sparkle in her eyes.

He watched those eyes widen when he tugged her close to him.

"You know," he said, circling her small waist with his hands, "there will never be another sunrise like this one."

Wary, she eased her head back and met his gaze. "Is that so?"

"That's so." When she started to pull away, he tightened his hold. "I've been up here dozens of times and every one was different."

She arched a dubious brow. "Different how?"

"Sometimes the sun jumps up like a giant mirror, so bright you can barely look at it." He angled his body against hers, tucked all those soft curves firmly against the hard length of his own. "Other times, it just sorta creeps up, slow and easy."

"Like a snake?"

"Maybe more like a storm," he said, grinning. "Some days up here you can even smell the clouds coming long before you see them." He lowered his head and breathed in the sweet scent of her. "Other days, all you can smell are the spring flowers."

He could see her pulse jumping at the base of her long neck, felt her tense in his arms. But still she didn't pull away.

"What—what kind of flowers?" she asked.

Lord, he wanted to kiss her, but she kept stalling. "Lupine, bluebonnets, primrose." He dropped his lips within a whisper of hers, until he felt her breath meet his. Damn, he was running out of flowers. "Flax, baby-blue eyes, fireweed…"

Oh, to hell with it.

He stopped trying to think and covered her mouth with his. Her lips were soft and warm and sweet as honey, and he traced them lightly with his tongue until she sighed and opened up to him. Sliding his hands up her back, he deepened the kiss, felt her tremble in his arms. He could lose himself in the incredible taste of her, and the thought almost had him pulling away. But need overrode reason and all he could do was pull her closer still.

It almost felt surreal, Alaina thought dimly. As if she were standing on top of the tallest mountain, in a warm cloud of desire. No one had ever kissed her like this before, made her mind go blank, until there was nothing but sensation after sensation rippling through her. Even though she'd known he would kiss her, maybe from the very first time she'd laid eyes on him, nothing could have prepared her for this rush of heat, for the sparks of sheer, intense pleasure. She could feel the sun on her face, hear the whisper of the breeze through the grass, the distant stomp of a horse's hoof. She melted into the kiss, into D.J., and afraid that her legs might give out, she slid her arms around his neck and held on.

He pulled her closer, fitted his body intimately with hers. She felt the hard press of his arousal between her legs, her breasts crushing against his broad, muscular chest. She met every hungry thrust of his tongue with her own, made a small sound deep in her throat, and he answered, then tightened his arms around her and crushed his mouth to hers. Excitement coursed through her veins, and she squirmed against him, needing to be closer still. Fire raced over her skin, and the rapid beat of her heart sounded like a drum in her head…

A drum?

What was happening to her? Why was her dream intruding? This was just a kiss, she told herself. An amazing kiss, but just a kiss. Her dream had no place here. Not with this man. It *couldn't*. But the fact that it had frightened her, brought her back to reality and had her jerking her head away.

"Wait." She struggled to get that simple word out. "I—I can't."

His arms tightened around her, and she was certain if he kissed her again, she would be completely lost. When he looked down at her, his eyes burning deep blue, it was all she could do not to drag his lips back to hers.

They were both still breathing hard as he stared at her, then his mouth flattened and he slowly loosened his hold. She stumbled back, pressed her fingertips to her lips, shocked at what she might have done. "I'm sorry."

His eyes narrowed. "For what?"

"I didn't mean to, I wasn't trying to—" Lord, she could barely say it. "Lead you on."

He raised a brow, studied her for what felt like hours, though it was only seconds, then he shook his head. "You're the damnedest woman, Alaina Blackhawk."

She had no idea what he meant by that, and she might have asked him, but he'd already turned and headed back to his horse. *Better to just leave it be,* she thought and followed after him.

The sun had been up at least an hour by the time D.J. and Alaina arrived back at the ranch. Baxter and Taffy greeted them with tongues rolling and excited barks. Though D.J. would have much preferred a quiet entrance, he knew there was no stopping those blasted dogs once they were riled up.

Several of the men were already in the corrals, and heads turned when they rode past. A few nodded, but they all knew better than to openly stare. For the short time she would be here, it would keep the hounds at bay, if they thought Alaina was his.

There was something about her, an innocence of sorts, that had both surprised and frustrated. There'd been a naïve sweetness about her, maybe in the way she'd trusted him, or that subtle shimmer of inexperience when his lips had first touched hers.

He wanted her, but she was a complicated woman, D.J. thought, and if there was one thing he didn't want, it was complications.

"Baxter!" D.J. shouted at the dog when he barked at Sergeant's back hooves. Damn dog was too stupid to realize that one kick from a twelve hundred pound horse could snap him like a twig. "Back off!"

Waving his hat, Bobby climbed over the corral fence and whistled for the dogs. They both ran toward the hand, yapping loudly and wagging their tails.

"Morning, boss." Bobby dropped his hat back on his head and smiled at Alaina. "I fed Santana for you and brushed him. Tried to check his hooves, but he got cross about it so I let it be."

"Thanks, Bobby." Alaina slid off Gypsy Belle. "But you really don't need to."

"I don't mind. I can walk him for you, too." Bobby looked at D.J. eagerly. "If that's okay with you, boss."

"Fine," D.J. said through gritted teeth, not sure what was more irritating, Bobby's sloppy grin or the dogs running circles around Alaina. "Take care of Sergeant and Gypsy first. And shut these damn mutts up."

"Yes, sir." Bobby grabbed both horses' reins and called the dogs, but when they spotted one of the hands driving into the yard, they raced to greet the newcomer.

Shaking his head, D.J. watched the dogs run in one direction while Alaina headed for the house and wondered how the hell, in less than twenty-four hours, he felt as if he'd lost complete control.

Six

"That's my sweetheart," Alaina crooned to Santana. "Come on now, you can do it. You know you can."

A saddle in her hands, she moved slowly toward the stallion. Head high and eyes wide, the horse watched her approach.

"I'm not going to hurt you, baby." She inched closer. "I would never hurt you."

Santana pricked his ears and tossed his head, but for the first time since she'd been working with him, the animal didn't try to back away.

"That's my big, brave boy," she murmured and positioned herself next to the horse. "Here we go now."

With one quick, smooth move, she swung the saddle onto the horse's back. He whinnied and pranced, but didn't rear. Elated, Alaina stroked the stallion's neck. She could feel the tension and energy coursing through Santana's muscles and she continued to murmur sweet nothings while she caressed his sleek coat.

"See, that's not so bad, now, is it?"

After two frustrating days of the animal immediately bucking the saddle off, this was a huge breakthrough. She waited for the horse to settle down again, then moved to the cinch and buckled it. Of course, she knew that while she may have won this particular battle, she was far from winning the war.

Which was exactly how she felt about her relationship with D.J.

Not that she had a *relationship* with the man. He'd kissed her, she'd kissed him back. End of story. She supposed they'd both simply been caught up in the moment of being alone, watching that amazing sunrise. No point in making a big deal about it, she told herself. It was just a kiss.

She hoped by the end of her two weeks here, she could convince herself of that.

No man had ever turned her inside out like that. Made her ache to be touched, to be loved. She'd tried to reason it was simply the magic of the moment, that she hadn't had enough sleep the night before, that she'd been vulnerable after the erotic dream that had been haunting her, then telling D.J. about her father.

But then she'd remember the feel of his lips on hers, the press of his hard body, and she knew it was so much more.

With a sigh, she smoothed a hand down the stallion's head. She'd managed to keep her distance from D.J. since that kiss, had kept busy working with Santana, and in the evening, with Dottie around, there wasn't much chance for a conversation, or for them to be alone, thank goodness. Being alone with D.J. was a dangerous thing. He was a man used to getting what he wanted, and he'd made it clear he wanted her. She'd seen him watching her for the past three days, had felt his gaze burn through her. Like the wolf, she thought. Waiting.

"All right, Al. You got a saddle on him."

She turned at the sound of Bobby's voice, saw the hand leaning over the stall door. He had a tendency to pop up several times during the day, whenever he wasn't busy with his regular ranch duties. "You doubted me?"

"Shoot, no." He grinned at her. "That stallion's an ornery one, but I knew he'd come around. You could sweet talk the thorns off a cactus."

"Thanks, I think." She smiled at the kid, knew that he had a little crush on her, though she'd been careful not to encourage him. It was nice that someone other than Dottie was talking to her, though, especially since the other men had kept their distance. Alaina knew she was the first woman to ever work on the Rocking B and more than likely the hands didn't approve of a female moving into their territory. It really didn't matter, whatever the reason was. She'd be gone by the end of next week, anyway.

"Dottie sent me to fetch you up to the house," Bobby said. "Wants you to come right away, if you can."

Alaina glanced at her wristwatch and frowned. It was already past five and she would have been going in soon, anyway, so it seemed odd that Dottie would ask for her. "Is there a problem?"

"Didn't say, but she tell me not to let D.J. know she was asking for you."

Not tell D.J.? Now that *was* odd, Alaina thought, and reached for the cinch on the stallion's saddle.

"You go on ahead." Bobby stepped into the stall. "I'll take care of Santana. We're buds now."

Alaina might have refused his offer if she didn't sense that something was wrong. Dottie wasn't the type to ask for help, so whatever it was, it must be important. "Thanks, Bobby. Ah, do you know where D.J. is?"

"Last I saw him, he was in the barn tack room with Judd."

Outside the stables, Alaina paused and glanced around. A couple of the men were working with a yearling in one of the corrals, and a couple more were unloading hay from a flatbed, but no sign of D.J. She headed for the utility room on the side of the house, scanned the yard before she ducked inside, pulled her boots and socks off, then opened the door and stuck her head inside the kitchen.

"Dottie?"

The room was empty, which was strange because the housekeeper was always cooking by this time. Alaina checked the downstairs, then called up from the bottom of the stairs.

"Up here," came a faint reply.

Worried, Alaina hurried up the stairs. "Where are you?"

"Here." Dottie's voice sounded out of breath. "In D.J.'s bedroom."

Alaina found the housekeeper in D.J.'s huge walk-in closet, sitting on the floor in the corner.

"What's wrong?" Alaina rushed to Dottie's side and knelt beside her. "Are you hurt?"

"No, no, no. I'm fine. It's the kittens." The woman picked up a flashlight, turned it on, then shined it into a small hole near the baseboards. "Three of them are inside the wall."

"What?" Alaina knelt down on the floor and peeked into the hole, saw two pairs of eyes shining back at her. "How did they get in there?"

"Esmeralda sneaked them into the closet, but they obviously found the hole on their own. She was cater-wauling so loud, I came up to see what happened."

"Where is she now?" Alaina asked.

"She wouldn't stay out of my way so I put her in my bathroom downstairs with the other two." Dottie sat back and swiped a hand across the beads of sweat on her brow. "My hand is too big to fit inside and I've been trying to entice them out for two hours, with no luck. I was hoping to get them out of here before D.J. comes in."

"Let me try."

When Dottie moved out of the way, Alaina lay down on the shiny hardwood floor and called to the kittens, but they didn't budge. Alaina slipped her hand into the hole up to her wrist, felt whiskers brushing against her fingertips, then reached her arm deeper into the wall and felt a paw. "Almost…"

She wiggled in farther and managed to wrap her hand around a tiny ball of soft fur. Smiling, she tried to pull it out.

And couldn't.

She struggled to free herself, but only seemed to make it worse. "I'm stuck."

"Oh, dear." Dottie looked at the hole, then shook her head and sighed. "No way around it, then. I'll go get a hammer."

"Wait—"

But Dottie had already hurried out and there was nothing Alaina could do but wait.

D.J. dropped his boots on the porch and limped in through the front door. Getting tossed off, stepped on, or kicked by a horse was pretty much a day in the life, but all three on the same day bruised more than a man's body.

Unbuttoning his shirt, he headed up the stairs. He'd intentionally bypassed the kitchen, was in no mood for Dottie fussing over him. He was hot and sweaty. All he wanted was a long, hot shower and an ice cold beer.

And a soft woman.

He frowned at the last thought. Thinking about a woman was what had caused him so much grief already. If he'd been paying more attention to his work instead of drifting off into lustful fantasies about Alaina, he wouldn't have an imprint of a hoof on his thigh. And if that hoof had been five inches to the left, he doubted he'd be thinking about *any* woman, let alone do anything else, for quite some time.

He shrugged his shirt off and tossed it on the bed, then pulled off his belt and unsnapped his jeans, was heading for the bathroom when he passed by the open door on his closet, stopped when he thought he heard a muffled voice coming from inside.

He stuck his head inside the closet, noticed several of his boots had been tossed into a pile, then noticed a pair of long, denim-clad, legs and bare feet stretched out on the floor.

Alaina?

He couldn't see beyond the pile of boots, but he could hear her whispering in a reassuring, calm tone, something about help on the way and don't worry.

What the hell...?

Moving into the closet, he could see her head was in the corner, her left arm folded against the wall, her right arm—past her elbow—inside a hole.

He knelt beside her, watched her body stiffen as her head slowly turned toward him.

"Hey, Alaina."

"Hey, D.J."

Unable to resist, he took a minute and scanned the length of her body. Her white tank top had risen and her jeans, cut low across her hips, revealed the bare skin on her lower back. He caught a hint of hot-pink underwear and something else that made his eyebrows lift.

"Never took you for the tattoo type," he said casually, could only see what looked like the tip of colorful butterfly wings, resisted the strong urge to tug her jeans lower and take a good look. Instead he allowed his gaze the pleasure of following the curve of her round bottom.

She wiggled and managed to turn on her side, pulling her tank top down. Which, of course, only drew D.J.'s attention to her breasts.

"I can explain—"

"The tattoo?" he asked. "Or why you're lying in my closet with your arm stuck in my wall?"

"The latter, or course." Her face was as pink as the polish on her toenails. "There's a kitten in your wall. Three, actually."

His bad mood and sore leg forgotten, he rocked back on one foot. "Is that what you say to all the men whose closets you sneak into?"

"I did *not* sneak in here," she protested. "Dottie—"

When she bit her lip, then pressed her lips firmly together, D.J. figured he had a pretty good idea of what had happened. "And where is Dottie?"

"She went to get a hammer."

He winced at the thought of his housekeeper with a hammer and started to rise.

"Where are you going?" she asked.

"To get my camera, of course."

Her hand reached out and grabbed his arm, latched on like a vise. "Don't you *dare!* Get back here and do something."

"Well, now, there's an invitation I can't refuse." Grinning, he lay down on his side and faced Alaina. "What would you like me to do?"

"Wipe that smile off your face for starters," she said tightly. "Then get my arm out of this damn hole."

"It's not every day a pretty girl gets her arm stuck in a hole in my closet." He propped his head on his bent arm, watched blue sparks fly out of her eyes. "I'm just savoring the moment."

"Dammit, Bradshaw, this isn't funny."

"You're kidding, right?"

"All right, so maybe it is," she said with a sigh. "But if you were a gentleman, you'd control yourself."

"Darlin', no one ever said I was a gentleman." He reached for a long strand of her hair that had fallen across her cheek and rubbed it between his forefinger and thumb. It felt like silk. "And at this moment, you can't even imagine the control I'm managing to exercise."

It seemed impossible to Alaina that—given the situation—she found herself responding to D.J.'s closeness. The fact that he was half-naked certainly contributed to the overwhelming presence of his body less than six inches from her own, not to mention that broad, muscled chest she couldn't seem to tear her eyes away from. Even the earthy scent of his bare skin, a mix of sweat and dust and horse, wasn't unappealing. If anything, she was…turned on.

"D.J., be serious." She considered pushing him away, but then she'd have to touch him and she wasn't certain she trusted herself. "Dottie will be back any minute."

"Remind you of high school?" he asked, lowering his voice. "Necking in the cab of your boyfriend's truck, worrying you'll get caught?"

"I wouldn't know," she admitted, then wished she hadn't.

"You don't?" He lifted a surprised brow, then lowered his head closer to hers. "Well, there's a lot of kissing going on, the we're-in-a-hurry kind."

When his lips nearly touched hers, Alaina held her breath. "D.J.—"

"Then there's some definite groping," he went on, and slid a fingertip along the waistband of her jeans. "Racing hormones. Hands all over the place."

How easy it was to imagine. The urgency, the thrill of danger, of excitement. Heavy breathing, steamed up windows, the struggle to maneuver steering wheel and cramped space. When D.J. lightly drew his finger back and forth over the tip of her butterfly wings, his touch burned through the fabric of her jeans, made her skin hot and tight. "Stop that," she whispered, but made no effort to brush his hand away.

"You gotta make me believe you," he murmured and circled the snap of her jeans with his finger. "I wouldn't make you do anything you didn't want to."

There was no doubt in Alaina's mind that D.J. never *had* to make a girl—or woman—do anything they didn't want to. Here she was, stuck in a wall, with Dottie about to walk in any minute, and all she could think about was D.J.'s lips almost touching hers and his finger one tiny tug away from opening her jeans.

Lord, I must be sick.

When the tip of his callused finger slipped under the hem of her tank top and slid—just barely—over her stomach, her pulse raced and her breath came in short, shallow gulps. She wanted his mouth on hers and she closed her eyes, parted her lips...

When D.J. rolled away, her eyes flew open. Disappointment and frustration coursed through her. She felt like kicking him, but without her boots on, she doubted the blow would have much impact. She watched him stand and pull a white T-shirt from a shelf.

"Dottie's coming." He slipped the T-shirt over his head and knelt down beside her again. "Put your head on the floor and don't move."

"What?" She stared at him, couldn't decide if he was kidding.

"Put your head on the floor," he repeated.

He wasn't kidding. "Why would I—"

She squeaked when he dropped one hand on her head and pressed her cheek to the floor, then raised his other hand. She squeezed her eyes shut when his fist came down over her head and punched a hole in the drywall.

"Why didn't you do that five minutes ago?" she said irritably and wiggled her arm loose.

"And miss all that fun?" He gave her a cocky smile and broke out another chunk of drywall. "Not a chance."

"You're right, Bradshaw." She frowned at him and scooted out of his way. "You are no gentleman."

Chuckling, he widened the hole and looked inside the wall as Dottie rushed into the closet, a hammer in one hand and a saw in the other. The housekeeper's eyes shifted from D.J. to the large, jagged hole in the wall, then set the tools on a shelf. "I, ah, guess we don't need those anymore."

D.J. threw Dottie a look over his shoulder, then reached into the hole, pulled out kitten number one, a calico.

Alaina took the kitten and stared into its tiny face. It squeaked out a mew. "Oh, you poor baby," Alaina cooed and laid the kitten in her lap. Kitten number two, black and white like its mama, came out next, blinking its big green eyes. Alaina laid the kittens in an empty shoe box and squeezed in closer to watch over D.J.'s shoulder.

"I'll go get Esmeralda." Dottie turned, then paused at the closet doorway, tears in her eyes. "You wonderful, wonderful man."

"So what do you think?" D.J. grinned at Alaina while he reached deeper into the wall for kitten number three. "Do you think I'm a—"

"What?" Alaina watched D.J.'s grin suddenly fade. "What's wrong?"

D.J.'s mouth hardened and he reached deeper into the wall. "This one's not moving."

Seven

D.J.'s gut tightened at the kitten's closed eyes and limp body. It was the pure white, long-haired runt of the litter and he knew it was Dottie's favorite. There were strands of fibers on the kitten's mouth. "He must have been sucking on the insulation."

Alaina reached for the kitten. "Let me have it."

D.J. shook his head. "I should take it before Dottie gets back."

"Just give it to me, D.J." she said urgently. Gently she removed the kitten from his hand and held it up to her ear. "There's a heartbeat, but it's faint."

"Alaina—"

"He'll be fine." She closed her eyes. "He'll be fine."

"The fiber glass—"

"Shh."

He watched her stroke the kitten, wanted to tell her to stop, to just let him handle it, but her determined expression held him at bay.

"Alaina, don't."

She didn't respond, and he narrowed his eyes, wasn't even certain that she heard him. Her fierce expression softened, her breathing slowed, and a calm smoothed her face. Gently she cradled the kitten in her hands, held it against her cheek. And still the kitten didn't move.

"Alaina," he whispered, but she didn't even seem to hear him. He dragged a hand through his hair, cursing his own feeling of helplessness and her stubborn refusal to face the obvious.

He reached to take the kitten from her, stopped at the sound of its tiny, screechy mew. The kitten's eyes slitted open, and it mewed again, this time a little stronger.

Son of a gun.

"Alaina." He touched her cheek with his thumb. Her eyelashes fluttered open and she looked around as if she didn't know where she was. "Are you all right?"

She stared at him for a long moment, blinked several times. Her lips slowly curved up. "He might be little, but he's a fighter."

Her smile lit her entire face and glowed in her eyes. He felt the warmth of it seep through him and lodge in his chest. "Yeah, I guess he is."

Esmeralda ran into the closet, sniffed her babies in the shoebox, then meowed loudly until Alaina placed the littlest ball of white fur into the shoebox beside its siblings.

Out of breath from running up the stairs, Dottie came into the closet, carrying the other two kittens. "Everything all right?"

"Fine." D.J. looked at Esmeralda. The cat was busy licking her kittens and she purred as loud as a motorboat. Grinning, he glanced back at Alaina. "It's just fine."

Alaina fell asleep after she took a shower and dressed. One minute she'd been sitting on the edge of her bed, getting ready to go downstairs for dinner, the next thing she knew it was dark. Confused, she glanced at the bedside clock, moaned when she saw it was eight-thirty.

Dammit, she should have known this would happen.

She sat on the side of the bed, pressed her fingers to her temple and waited for the room to stop spinning. Her mind was still groggy and thick, her vision blurred, but she knew that would pass shortly. It always did.

Dragging her hands over her hair, she stood slowly and tested her legs. When they held her, she made her way to the door and stepped out into the hallway, was heading for the stairs when the light from D.J.'s open office door caught her attention. If he was anything like Trey—and he was—she assumed he didn't like to be bothered when he was in his "cave." But she was embarrassed she'd fallen asleep, not just through dinner, but for the past three hours. She at least owed him—and Dottie—an apology.

Biting her lip, she moved closer to the open door and looked inside.

He sat behind a large mahogany desk, his tall frame

hunkered down in a high-back, brown leather chair while he stared intently at a computer screen. His hair looked wet and uncombed, as if he'd just showered and pulled a T-shirt over his head. Her heart thumped and she looked away, needed a minute to gather her wits.

The room was floor-to-ceiling bookshelves, she noted, every shelf filled to overflowing. A football trophy had been carelessly squeezed into a corner and a cow skull stared blindly from its place on top of a pile of ranching periodicals. But it was the telescope sitting on a tripod in front of a pair of wide windows that had her lifting a brow.

"I wouldn't have taken you for a man who liked to look at the stars."

He glanced up, pressed a button to clear his monitor, then dropped his head back against his chair and met her gaze. "Sleeping beauty awakes."

Blushing, she stayed in the doorway. "Sorry to bother you."

"You're saving me. If I have to balance one more column on one more account, I think I might shoot myself." He stretched his legs out, crossed one booted ankle over the other. "You okay?"

"I'm fine. It was just a headache." She couldn't really explain it any other way. "I'm sorry I didn't come down for dinner."

"Dottie checked in on you before she left, but you were sleeping so soundly she didn't want to wake you."

Alaina frowned. "Dottie left?"

"Her daughter, Velma, called a little while ago." D.J.

picked up a mug of coffee on his desk and sipped. "She went into labor early."

"Oh." Alaina chewed on her lower lip. She and D.J. were alone, she realized, truly alone, and the thought made her shoulders tense. "I hope she and the baby are all right."

"She would have called if there were any problems." He sipped on the coffee again. "She left a plate of food for you in the fridge. You hungry?"

She looked at D.J., the long stretch of legs, his damp, mussed hair, those broad shoulders, and she had to swallow before she could speak. "Maybe later. I thought I'd check on the kittens."

"I've banished them to the laundry room," he said. "Hopefully they can stay out of trouble in there."

"Did you check for holes?" Alaina asked, smiling.

"Oh, yeah. Here, sit." He rose from his chair, sat on the edge of his desk. "How'd you do with Santana today?"

Santana. Between all the commotion this afternoon, then falling asleep, she'd nearly forgotten. Needing to keep some distance between herself and D.J., she bypassed the chair he'd offered, shoved her hands into the front pockets of her jeans and wandered the room. "I got a saddle on him today."

D.J. nodded. "That's progress."

"He's still a little unhappy with the situation, but I think he might let me ride him tomorrow." She glanced over the books on D.J.'s shelves. He had everything from land management to horse training to veterinarian medicine, not to mention several shelves of classics and current, bestselling novels. So the man liked to read, she thought with interest and spotted an older Dick Francis novel. She pulled it from the bookshelf and opened it, noted the tattered book cover and dog-eared pages. "I loved this one."

"I haven't read it." He stared at his coffee, then set the cup on his desk. "It was my mother's."

"Oh." He'd never once mentioned his parents, though she'd heard both Cookie and Dottie say their death had been a shame. "What happened?" she asked softly. "To her and your dad?"

He was quiet for a long moment, stared out the window into the dark night, and she was certain she'd stepped into territory he simply didn't want to discuss.

She closed the book and slipped it back on the shelf. "I'll just go check on the—"

"A fire," he said, his voice distant. "We lived in a smaller house where the front pasture is now. It was already here when my parents moved here forty years ago, but my dad had always wanted something bigger for my mom, so he built this one for her. Since she'd never been able to have more children after me, she entertained instead. I hated those parties we had at the old house and all the ones she dragged me to. My mom loved them."

Alaina watched D.J.'s eyes soften, then he dragged his fingers through his hair and sighed. "Took them five years to build this one, another year to decorate and furnish. When it was finally done, we packed up the rest of our things and moved everything over to the new house, but my mom wanted to stay one last night in the old one. She talked about the past, made my dad and me go through her old photo albums after dinner, said she didn't want me to forget where I'd come from. My dad talked about the future, how we were going to build the biggest and the best horse ranch in the state."

Alaina had no memories of both her parents, only her mother lighting candles every night under a photo of the man who'd abandoned her and her children. "That sounds like a wonderful evening."

A muscle jumped in D.J.'s jaw. and he slowly shook his head. "I was sixteen, bored and annoyed because school had just let out and there was this cute little redhead who liked to hang out at the pool hall in town. Last thing I wanted to do was sit at home with my parents. I kept grumbling about it, so my mom finally told me to go have some fun. She didn't need to tell me twice. I was out of there and on my way to town like a bullet. It was just past midnight when I got back and saw the flames and everyone running around. The hands had managed to drag my parents out before the roof went up, but the smoke had already overtaken them. They died in their bed."

He blamed himself, Alaina realized. She could see it in his eyes, could *feel* it. She wanted to tell him not to, but she knew it wouldn't matter, knew that he'd made the decision to accept fault. No one could change that decision but himself.

"Cleaning rags," he said, leveling a gaze at Alaina. "A big pile of goddammed cleaning rags."

"I'm so sorry." She knew the words would sound

empty to D.J., but she said them anyway. She wanted to go to him and put her head on his shoulder, but she could see the stiffness in his shoulders, the tight set of his face and knew that her comfort would not be welcomed.

The silence stretched around them, long and dark, heavy, and when the shrill ring of the phone finally broke that quiet, Alaina jumped.

"Hey, Dottie." D.J. looked up, met Alaina's worried gaze while he listened. "Uh, huh…no kidding…you don't say…all right…sure."

Chewing on a fingernail, she moved closer to D.J., grateful for Dottie's timing. She could hear the buzz of the housekeeper's voice, though, and Alaina craned her neck to listen, hoping to catch a few words.

"Here, tell her yourself."

Without warning, D.J.'s arm reached out and slid around her waist. Alaina squeaked when he pulled her between his legs and held the phone up to her ear.

"You all right?" Dottie asked.

Lord, she couldn't breathe, let alone think straight with D.J.'s thighs pressing against hers. He held onto the phone, forcing her head close to his if she wanted to hear. "I—yes, I'm fine," she choked out, laid a hand on D.J.'s chest to prevent him from pulling her against him. "How—how's your daughter?"

Between the roar of the blood pumping in her head and Dottie talking so fast, Alaina could barely hear, but she managed to pick up enough words to know that mother and daughter—Alyssa Anne, six pounds, seven ounces—were doing very well.

"That's wonderful." Alaina struggled to keep her voice even, sucked in a breath when D.J. slowly, but insistently, drew her closer. She could feel the rapid beat of his heart under her palm, smell the fresh scent of soap on his skin. She knew Dottie was saying something about the birthing process, but Alaina couldn't have kept the words straight if her life depended on it. How could she possibly think, or breathe, standing between D.J.'s legs, his hand moving over the small of her back, his mouth so close to hers she'd barely have to lean forward for their lips to touch?

She couldn't, she realized, but even more frightening, was the fact that she didn't want to think or breathe or move away.

Lifting her eyes to D.J.'s, Alaina saw the need burning there, knew that it mirrored her own. His gaze sharpened, then lowered to her mouth. Anticipation trembled through her, buzzed in her head.

She looked at the phone, realized the buzzing she heard was the dial tone.

"She hung up."

"Yeah." Keeping his eyes on her mouth, D.J. took the phone and replaced it on the cradle. "She did."

"Oh." He had both hands around her waist now and that single word was the best she could manage.

"I should tell you." His thumbs stroked the small of her back. "I lied to you."

"You did?" *Two words.* Better, she thought.

He dropped his mouth closer to hers. "I wasn't really working tonight."

"No?" Damn. Back to one word.

He shook his head. "I was thinking about you."

"Me?"

"Pretty hard to keep my mind on work, when I'm thinking about what you look like when you're sleeping." His arms tightened around her, drew her closer. "All I could see was you, lying on your back, with that incredible hair of yours streaming across your pillow."

Heat flooded her veins, ran like a molten river through her body. She felt a moment of panic, as if she'd been caught in a trap. But the moment passed, and she knew that if she truly wanted to stop this, she could.

God help her, she didn't want to.

Breath held, she waited, watched his head lower to hers, felt the warmth of his breath, smelled the clean scent of his soap. When his lips finally touched hers, her eyes fluttered closed.

He tasted like rich, dark coffee, with all the potent kick that had her nerves jangling and sprinting at the same time. She heard a sound, an animal-like moan, and realized it came from deep in her throat. His mouth was hard and firm, familiar to her now, but more demanding than the kiss on the mesa, more impatient. But she was impatient, too, and she strained against him, wanting more.

She'd been so cautious her entire life, afraid to truly let herself go, to let herself *feel* without restraint. There were risks involved. Her dream had warned her of that. But at this moment, the only thing that mattered was being here, with D.J. She melted into him, felt her knees grow weak. Afraid she might slip through his arms, she held onto him, shivering with pleasure.

Hurry, she thought, but didn't want to take her mouth away from his to tell him. So she told him with her hands, raced her fingers down his neck, over the hard muscles of his shoulders. She'd felt that broad chest earlier, without his shirt, and she wanted her hands on his skin again, this time unfettered. Uninterrupted.

Blood pumped like a fist through D.J.'s body, hot and hard and fast. He'd known there was heat simmering under Alaina's carefully controlled surface, but he'd never expected it to slam into him like a two-by-four. He feasted on her mouth, tasted the honey sweetness of her, and the little sounds she made in her throat drained all the blood from his brain and sent it south. He dragged his mouth from hers, fisted his hands in her silky hair and tugged her head back, blazing kisses down the smooth column of her neck. He felt her pulse skip under his tongue and he savored the heat of her soft skin, nipped at the intoxicating taste. Her moan vibrated through him, and the urgency, the need, tightened inside him like a coiled spring.

He was close to losing it, dangerously, foolishly close, and the soft sounds she made, her whispered pleas, nearly pushed him over the edge. He could take her here, he realized. Right here, right now. The floor, the desk—hell, he didn't care. But he'd never prepared for anything like this, not even in his wildest fantasies, and while he could still hold himself together, he needed to get her to his bed.

When she moved her hips against him, sweat beaded on his forehead.

On an oath, he wrapped his arms around her and crushed her to him as he stood, lifting her off the floor.

"Bed," he choked out.

"Yes," she murmured, then locked her mouth on his again.

He carried her to his bedroom, worried more than once they might not make that short distance. Her soft breasts pressed against his chest and he had to remind himself to breathe. He needed to touch her, needed her naked and underneath him, needed her legs wrapped around him.

Like a beacon, moonlight slanted through the windows, casting a silver glow across his bed. Together they tumbled across the bedspread, and he rose above her, slid his hand down her throat, felt her pulse jumping under his fingers. Her face glowed in the pale light; her eyelids, heavy with desire, fluttered open. She met his gaze, held it when she reached for the hem of her tank top and pulled it off. He caught her arms before she could lower them again, circled her wrists with his hands and pinned them over her head. Her breasts, full and round, enclosed in white satin, rose and fell with her labored breathing. The glorious sight of her, her lips swollen with his kisses, her body writhing under him, aroused him to the point of pain.

"I've wanted my hands on you from the first moment I saw you," he said, his lungs nearly bursting. "Thought about you here, like this."

"Like this?" she whispered, lifting her hips against his.

He swore his heart stopped just before it slammed against his ribs. Lightning quick, he rolled to his back, caught her gasp with his mouth, kissed her until she melted over him. "Just like that," he murmured. "And like this."

The thrill of his hands on her breasts ignited sparks of white-hot pleasure through her body. She couldn't think, could only feel. Sensation after sensation spiraled through her, tightened like a fist. Every hurried brush of lips, every caress, was filled with brilliant, swirling colors. Wanting, needing more, she rushed her hands under his T-shirt, and the heat of his hard, muscled stomach vibrated through her fingertips like an electrical current.

"Your shirt," she gasped, sliding her hands up his broad chest. "Off."

And then they were rolling again, arms and legs tangling. Satin shimmered to the floor, boots dropped. She reeled from the intensity of the force driving her, and when his mouth dropped to her bare breast, when his tongue swept hot and moist over her beaded nipple, she arched upward on a moan. He teased with his teeth and lips, and when he drew her into his mouth and suckled, an arrow of fire shot straight from her breast to the throbbing ache between her thighs.

His mouth trailed hot kisses down her stomach at the same time he reached for the snap of her jeans and flicked it open. She heard the hiss of her zipper, felt the denim slide down her hips while his mouth moved lower still. He trailed kisses along the hollow of her hip while he tugged her jeans off and tossed them aside. She clutched at his shoulders and shivered when he slid a fingertip along the elastic band of her panties, then slipped underneath and stroked the most intimate part of her.

She moved against him, was certain she couldn't stand anymore, that she might die from pleasure this intense. "Please," she moaned. "D.J., please…I need you…"

He slid her panties off in one swift move, and when he moved away from her, she moaned in protest and opened her eyes, watched him unsnap his jeans and tug them off. He kept his eyes on her and the look on his face, fierce and primal, made her heart jump wildly. The sight of him standing over her, his broad shoulders and lean waist, his arousal, took her breath away. Excitement and fear and need coursed through her blood.

It took him but a moment to protect himself and when he turned back to her, his eyes glinting, his muscles taut, her breath shuddered from her lungs. He lowered his body to hers, slid his hands down her thighs and spread her legs, then drove himself inside her. And froze.

Eyes wide, he lifted his head, stared at her. "What…?"

"Don't stop." Afraid he might pull away, she wound her arms around his neck and held him tight.

"Alaina—"

"Don't stop," she pleaded, lifting her hips up, taking him deeper inside her. "Please."

"But you—" When she moved her hips again, he swore. "God, why didn't you—"

She dragged his mouth to hers and wrapped her legs

around him, letting instinct drive her. Need pounded through her, consumed her, and she heard him swear again, then grasp hold of her hips and move inside her, slowly at first, then faster, deeper. She met him thrust for thrust, gasping, frantic, until the need burst into flames and exploded inside her, showering sparks of red and gold. She floated with the embers, held on tight when D.J. groaned deep in his throat, then shuddered violently. Smiling, she sank back into the warm waves still rippling through her and let them carry her away.

At thirty-four, D.J. had thought nothing would shock him. Had thought nothing would surprise, or catch him off guard. He'd seen a lot, experienced a lot, considered himself well prepared to handle anything that came along.

Until now.

He held Alaina in his arms, too stunned to speak, wouldn't even know what to say if he could find his voice. The woman had quite simply devastated him, and the fact that she was a virgin—that utterly confused him. No woman had ever done that to him before—devastated or confused.

He pressed his lips to her forehead, then rolled to his side and pulled her with him. "Are you—did I—"

She stopped him with a kiss. "You were wonderful," she whispered. "That was wonderful."

"Yeah?" In spite of the guilt nipping away at him, he couldn't stop the swell of smug satisfaction. "Well, for a beginner, you were pretty damn wonderful yourself."

"Was I? Really?" She looked up at him, a mixture of

hope and uncertainty in her eyes. "'Cause you don't have to say that, I mean, I appreciate the gesture, but—"

He flipped her onto her back so quickly, she hadn't time to utter a squeak before his mouth was on hers. He kissed her, hard and long, until her arms came around his neck and he could feel her body humming under his.

"I assure you, Miss Blackhawk," he said against her mouth. "That was no gesture. You were incredible."

Her lips curved into a smile. "Thank you," she murmured, sliding her hands down his back. "You made it…special."

He'd made it special? Good God, he thought about what had just happened, what she'd given him—and done to him—and knew there were no words. He lifted his head and gazed down at her. "You could have told me."

"I could have." Her eyes slowly opened. "And maybe if the circumstances were different, if we'd been dating, or I'd known this was going to happen, I might have."

"But tonight—"

She put her fingers on his mouth. "What if I had told you? Would it have changed anything?"

Would it? he asked himself. Maybe he would have resisted her, backed off. Done the right thing. Oh, hell. Who was he kidding?

"No." He sighed and pressed his lips to her fingertips. "But I would have been more careful."

"If I wanted careful, I would have gone back to my bedroom, alone." Shyly she dropped her gaze, ran her fingers over his jaw and down his neck. "I'm glad I didn't."

"That makes two of us." But he was still reeling from

what had just happened between them, still trying to understand. "I look at you and see a beautiful, exciting woman, and I'm seriously wondering what's wrong with all the men in your town."

"There's nothing wrong with the men," she said quietly. "I'm the one who—"

When she stopped, he tucked a finger under her chin and lifted her head until she met his gaze. "Who what?"

She hesitated, then shrugged one shoulder. "Let's just say it was my choice."

"Alaina—"

"Bradshaw, stop." She frowned at him. "Just stop right there and get rid of the I-just-ran-over-a-puppy look. I'm twenty-seven, and maybe that's old by most people's standards, but dammit, I waited because I wanted my first time to be right, to *feel* right. It did, and it does. I have no expectations, and you have no accountability. We are two mature, consenting adults, and don't you go and ruin this with some misguided sense of guilt."

Surprised by her outburst, he stared down at the firm press of her mouth and the indignant glint in her eyes. Would this woman never cease to amaze him? he wondered. When she pushed at his shoulders to move him off her, he stayed put.

"Did anybody ever tell you that you're sexy when you're naked and mad?" he asked.

She stilled at his words, then looked up at him with surprise. "You think I'm sexy?"

He dropped a kiss to her lips. "Lady, if you were any sexier, I'd be in the hospital."

She arched a brow. "The hospital, huh?"

"ICU."

"You don't say." Her smile was angelic, but he saw the devil in her eyes when she slid her hands slowly up his arms. "So how far is the hospital from here?"

She raised up and moved her lips over his, a slow, thorough kiss that sucked the breath from his lungs and every thought from his brain. When she arched her hips upward, the heat, and the urgency, surged once again and the force of it staggered him. Unsettled him.

But the soft feel of her body under his, the silky slide of her arms over his shoulders, swooped over him and gripped hold with talonlike claws. He wrapped his arms tightly around her, felt the need overtake him, and he brought her with him.

Eight

The sun stretched hot and hard across the late morning blue sky, laid down heavy with the scent of horse, baked dirt and sweat. From the barn, the persistent clang of hammer on anvil rang out on the thick summer air, while Baxter and Taffy barked lazily at men riding in from the outer pastures.

His arms draped over a fence post, D.J. watched Alaina trot Santana around the inside of the corral. It was the third day she'd ridden the stallion, the first day the horse hadn't been determined to pitch her off. But as stubborn and cantankerous as Santana could be, Alaina had refused to back down even once. She'd been patient and calm, unfaltering, always seemed to know when to be firm, or when to back off and give the horse his head.

She was one hell of a woman. And for the moment, she was his.

He liked waking up with Alaina in his arms. Liked the way her lashes fluttered just before she opened them, the way she stretched that long, curvy body. The way her soft blue eyes would meet his, then darken with desire when he pulled her underneath him. *Damn,* he liked that.

He'd taken her to his bed every night since that first time, and every night, she continued to surprise him, not only with her eagerness, but with her fiery sensuality. When she'd told him she was making up for lost time, he told her he had to be the luckiest man in the world.

During the day they kept their distance from each other, barely even spoke to each other, but the minute they were in the house, well, they didn't talk a whole lot then, either, he thought with a smile.

"She's a hot one."

D.J.'s smile turned to a frown when Judd leaned against the fence beside him. "What the hell did you say?"

"Easy there, boy, I was talking about the weather." Judd tipped his hat back and looked at Alaina. "But since you mentioned it—"

"Shut up," D.J. snapped.

Well, now." Grinning, Judd glanced back at D.J. and lifted a brow. "Isn't this interesting? D.J. Bradshaw, riled up over a woman."

"Like hell I am." To prove it, D.J. kept his fist at his side. "Haven't you got something to do?"

"Nope." Enjoying himself now, Judd touched the

brim of his hat when Alaina cantered past. "Looks as good coming as going."

D.J.'s lip curled. "You trying to provoke me?"

"I'm talking about Santana," Judd said innocently. "Damn, you're sensitive. So it's serious, then, is it?"

"I don't know what you're talking about."

"Sure you do."

Because he knew that Judd was like a dog with a bone when something was on his mind, D.J. just shrugged. "No, it's not serious."

"So it's just sex?"

Because Judd had prepared himself for it, he managed to stop the fist that D.J. threw at his jaw. "Simmer down, son. Just wanted to know if your intentions are honorable."

Eyes narrowed, D.J. jerked his arm from Judd's grasp. "None of your damn business."

"Something wrong?"

D.J. looked up, had been too focused on Judd to realize that Alaina had reined in Santana a few feet away. *Dammit, anyway.* He hoped like hell she hadn't heard any of the exchange between himself and his foreman. "Nothing's wrong."

"Heat makes some men downright surly." Judd winked at Alaina. "Lookin' good, darlin'."

D.J. swore silently and gritted his teeth. In spite of the irritation clenching his jaw, D.J. watched Alaina slide her hand over Santana's neck and couldn't stop the raw hunger that surged through his blood. And just thinking about what those fingers felt like on his skin sent all that blood south.

"He is, isn't he?" Alaina smiled. "He's still got quite a temper, but we're working on it."

"He'll settle down." Judd cocked a grin at D.J., which earned him a dark scowl. "Soon as he figures out he can't have everything his way."

"Well, he better hurry up about it." Alaina held tight on the reins when the horse tossed his head and pawed a hoof. "We haven't got much time."

D.J. saw the amusement in his foreman's eyes, vowed to seriously hurt the other man when they were alone. *Were his intentions honorable?* He thought about Stone Ridge Stables, about the offer to buy the ranch that was sitting on his desk, told himself that sleeping with Alaina had no influences on his business deals.

"I thought I'd ride into town this afternoon." Alaina glanced at D.J. "Santana could use a break and Bobby tells me you have a good livery in Bridle Peak."

His first reaction was to tell her she sure as hell *wasn't* going to Bridle Peak on a Saturday, when more than half the local cowboys came into town looking for a cold brew and female companionship.

"I can send one of the men," he offered casually. "Just tell me what you need."

"Not necessary," Alaina said. "I'd like to check it out myself, and I thought I'd walk around town a bit."

When the stupid grin on Judd's face widened, it was all D.J. could do not to knock it off. Dammit, he'd had enough of the man's nonsense. He could think whatever he damn well pleased.

"Fine," D.J. said through gritted teeth and pushed away from the fence. "I'll go with you."

D.J. was quiet on the hour long ride into Bridle Peak, and Alaina sensed that he wasn't exactly excited to be going to town. Still, with the air-conditioning on high, Shania Twain singing "I Feel Like a Woman" on the radio and the seemingly endless, but majestic landscape stretching out from the highway, she was enjoying the change of pace and scenery too much to let his terse silence spoil her good mood.

It wasn't as if she hadn't done her best to discourage him from going with her. Before she'd gone into the house to shower she'd told him straight out she'd *rather* go by herself, that she wanted to do some shopping. She'd figured that would have placed almost as high on the eight-letter-words-to-send-men-running scale as weddings and marriage.

But it hadn't, and he'd come into the house just as she was strapping on her sandals, taken one look at her dressed in her white blouse and pink skirt, then given her a look that scorched her from the tips of her bare toes to the top of her still damp hair. Because she'd known that all he'd have to do was reach for her and they'd end up in the bedroom instead of going to town, she'd quickly retreated to the laundry room to play with the kittens.

That's all it took to make her knees weak or her pulse race—a heated look or a subtle brush of his fingers. It still shocked her how uninhibited she'd become when making love with D.J., how wanton.

She'd wondered if all women felt so completely over-whelmed by the experience, so absolutely consumed. Except for Alexis, she'd never discussed the subject of sex with another woman, and even then, Alaina had listened more than she'd actually talked. Alexis had made it sound exciting, but she'd never said that it turned you inside out and shook you apart. That it made you ache and it made you yearn.

She'd gone willingly into D.J.'s arms—and to his bed—that first night. And she'd gone willingly every night since. She refused to allow herself to consider the possibility of any kind of future relationship with him, just as she refused to think about any kind of future without him. She'd let that pain come later. Now, it was so much simpler not to think at all, but to simply be in the moment and let herself feel.

The sound of a horn honking snapped her out of her thoughts and she realized the truck had slowed and they'd already turned off the highway and were entering into town. She glanced back at the truck that had passed them and saw a friendly arm waving out of the driver's window.

Bridle Peak looked pretty much like any other small Texas town, she thought, noting the two-story brick buildings with the usual mix of quaint mom and pop businesses, the slow stroll of Saturday afternoon shoppers, the dusty pickup trucks and weathered cowboys. Still, as similar as so many of the towns were, they each had their own individual charm, their own culture and history, and it was always fun to explore a new place. She noticed a gallery of local artists and a wildlife museum, then a cute little gift store with a jewel-toned shawl in the window that would look nice on her mother. "You can just drop me off here."

D.J.'s hands tightened on the steering wheel, and he pulled sharply into a parking space and practically slammed on the brake. "You trying to get rid of me?"

The irritation in his tone, not to mention his erratic driving, startled her. "What are you talking about?"

"First you tried to talk me out of coming with you, now you want me to drop you off." Jaw set, he frowned. "I'd say that's trying to get rid of me."

"You're the one who's been pawing sod since I said I was going to town." Good Lord, and they said *women* were moody. "You obviously didn't want to come, so why did you?"

"Why did you get all dressed up to come look at a livery?"

"What?" She glanced down at her simple white blouse and plain pink skirt, then looked back at him, stunned. "You came to town with me because of the way I'm dressed?"

A muscle jumped at the corner of his eye. "I didn't say that."

"So what are you saying?"

"Not a damn thing." He pulled his hat lower on his head, got out of the truck and came around to open the passenger door. "I'll be at Sawyer's. Be there at six."

He slammed the door shut after she slid out, then walked away without so much as a backward glance. She stared after him, bewildered by his strange behavior. And then the thought struck her, had her furrowing her brow.

Was he *jealous?*

No, she shook her head and laughed at herself. He couldn't be. Certainly not because she'd wanted to come to town, or because she'd put on a skirt. It wasn't even a short skirt, for heaven's sake—if anything, it covered more than it showed.

Frowning, she watched those broad shoulders of his disappear into the barber shop. What was he thinking, that she'd come to town "dressed up" so she could flirt with other men? She was torn between being insulted and being thrilled.

She decided to go with the thrilled.

Glancing at her wristwatch, she realized she didn't have much time. She didn't know who or what Sawyer's was, but she'd find out. In the meantime, she'd come to town with a plan, and she had no intention of allowing D.J.'s bad mood deter her.

"So this fool here is so plowed, he's singing Be My Baby Tonight to a cow."

From his corner booth, D.J. glanced over at Tommy Hunt, a local ranch hand who'd been loudly telling the story to the other men gathered around Sawyer's new pool table. Tommy dug a cell phone out of the front pocket of his jeans.

"God bless the man who invented cell phones with cameras," Tommy said and held the picture up, eliciting cheers and laughter from the other men.

"How do you know it wasn't a woman who invented it?" Missy, Tommy's girlfriend said, thrusting one curvy hip out.

"Too many buttons to push." Tommy pointed the camera at Missy's abundant breasts and took a picture, which brought forth a new round of laughter.

"Yeah, well, I certainly knew which buttons to push last night, didn't I, Tommy, baby?" Missy shot back, and all the men howled and clinked their beer bottles.

D.J. had done his best to ignore the rambunctious group since he'd walked in almost an hour ago, had politely shrugged off the ranch hands attempts to draw him in. He knew most of them, knew they were pretty harmless and any other time, he might have joined them for a quick beer. But he wasn't in the mood for their fool-ishness today, and if he'd had any idea that Sawyer's had recently added a pool table and two pinball machines, giving the restaurant more of a tavern environment, he never would have told Alaina to meet him here.

And where the hell was she? he wondered, taking a pull on the bottle of beer he'd ordered. It was nearly six-thirty, dammit. She should have been here thirty minutes ago.

While he tapped his fingers on the wooden tabletop and waited for her, he glanced at the bull riding event on the TV over the bar, watched a rider hang on to one big, mean looking bull for six seconds before he got tossed, then stomped on until the rodeo clowns drew the furious animal away.

He stared at the front entrance to the restaurant and frowned. So she was late. So what? It wasn't as if Bridle

Peak was exactly a hot spot for crime, for crying out loud. It was perfectly safe to walk around town by yourself, day or night, and the place wasn't big enough to get lost for long. He had no reason to be worried. Alaina was a big girl, and he was sure she was capable of taking care of herself. D.J. took another sip of beer as a new round of rowdy laughter from Tommy and his friends burst forth, making him wonder how many randy cowboys were walking around town right now, no doubt salivating over that pretty little lady in the pretty pink skirt.

The thought had his hand tightening on his beer. What the hell was wrong with him? He'd never been this bothered over a woman before, never had his insides knot up on him wondering where she was, what she was doing. He knew he'd overreacted when he'd stomped off earlier and left her standing by the truck, but when she'd asked him to drop her off, something had just snapped.

He'd never snapped before, dammit.

He tried to tell himself that he just felt responsible for her, that's all. He'd asked her to come to his ranch, he'd agreed not to tell her brother that she was staying at the Rocking B. If he felt unusually protective, it was because he'd taken her virginity, and he couldn't help but feel accountable for her safekeeping while she was at his ranch.

But every excuse had fallen as hard and as flat as that bull rider on the TV, and he felt as if he was getting stomped on by his own damn ignorance. It was more than that, and he knew it was more than that.

He cared for her—he cared *about* her. The feelings he had were unfamiliar to him, and he'd tried to explain them away because they made him nervous. He didn't like being nervous, he thought irritably. And he sure as hell didn't like caring this much.

The beer he'd lifted stopped halfway to his mouth when she walked in the door. And so did his heart.

Her cheeks were flushed from the heat outside and she'd clipped her thick mane of hair onto her head, exposing the long, delicate column of her neck. Her eyes had a smoky look to them, her lips were glossy pink. The light behind her created a silhouette of her slender body and his throat turned to sawdust at the sight.

He watched her glance around the room until she spotted him, then she moved toward him, several shopping bags in her hands and a smile on her face.

Except for the low volume on the TV, the room had quieted and D.J. quickly looked over at the group of young ranch hands. Eyes wide, slack-jawed, they all stared openly at Alaina, watched her stroll across the restaurant and slide into the booth across from D.J. When the men saw who she was sitting with, every pair of eyes met D.J.'s. The fiery look he narrowed back had the men quickly looking away.

"Sorry I'm late." She settled her bags on the seat beside her. "I lost track of time."

D.J. set his teeth. He'd been sitting here staring at the clock and she'd lost track of time? He swore silently and tossed back the rest of his beer, then smacked the bottle down on the table. "Let's go."

"Go?" Her brow furrowed. "I thought we were eating here."

"It's not that good." He threw a couple of dollars on the table and started to rise. "There's another place you'll like better."

"This place is fine, and it smells wonderful." She picked up a menu and settled back in the booth. "Everyone I talked to said this was the best barbecue in the entire county and their tri-tip is to die for."

Reluctantly D.J. sat back down and glanced at the ranch hands again, caught of couple of them sneaking looks at Alaina. Someone just *might* die, he thought, glaring at the men until they looked away.

He was trying to come up with another excuse to leave when Stacy, the waitress appeared and slid two glasses of water on the table. He had dated the pretty blonde in high school a couple of times when she'd been on the cheerleading squad. She was married now with two kids and quite obviously another on the way. Curiosity all but dripped when she glanced quickly at Alaina, then turned her attention back to him.

"Long time no see, D.J.," Stacy said. "How's it going?"

"Fine." Any other time, he would have shot the bull with Stacy. Today, all he wanted to do was order, eat and get the hell out. Stacy, on the other hand, appeared to be in no hurry at all. Because he knew that the woman would keep the chitchat going at least until she got an introduction, D.J. nodded at Alaina. "This is Alaina Blackhawk."

"Stacy." The waitress offered a hand and smiled. "I heard a woman trainer hired on at D.J.'s ranch. That you?"

"I'm just here for a few days." Smiling back, Alaina took the woman's hand. "When is your baby due?"

"Eight weeks." Stacy smoothed a hand over her protruding stomach. "He's kicking so darn much we've already nicknamed him Bronco."

Oh God, no. D.J. gritted his teeth and tamped down the threatening groan. No baby talk, *please* no baby talk.

But he might as well have tried to stop the sun from rising or setting, and while Stacy went on to describe her last two deliveries and then pulled out pictures of the little darlings, D.J. gritted his teeth and made an effort to be polite. He decided if he'd been given a choice, he'd take the ranch hands lascivious staring over Stacy's chatter about diapers and teething.

But since he didn't have a choice, D.J. mentally sighed and settled back in the booth, listened to the clack of pool balls and clinking beer glasses while he watched another bull rider on the TV get thrown, then pop back up and run before the bull could crush him.

After what felt like ten hours instead of ten minutes, Stacy finally pulled her order pad out of the pocket of her black skirt. "So what are you two having?"

"I heard your tri-tip is good." Alaina looked at the menu. "But the barbecued chicken sounds good, too."

"Bring her both." Before she could change her mind or the women took another ten minutes to discuss chicken versus tri-tip, D.J. took the menu and handed it to the waitress. "I'll have the same."

"You want four dinners?" Stacy asked, raising a brow.

Alaina frowned at him. "D.J.—"

"I'm hungry," he said evenly. "We'll take home what's left,"

"You're the boss." But Stacy shook her head as she wrote the order. "Drinks?"

Alaina ordered a margarita with salt and he ordered another bottle of beer. When Stacy walked away, Alaina leaned back in her seat and folded her arms, then arrowed a look of utter exasperation at him.

"What?"

"Don't give me that," she said coolly. "You're jumping around in your seat like a three-legged grasshopper."

He frowned at her analogy, reached casually for the beer he'd been nursing the past hour and finished off the last warm swallow. "I don't know what you're talking about."

"Tell you what," she said and started to scoot out of the booth. "You see if you can figure out what's eating you while I go play a game of pinball."

He reached out and grabbed her arm with lightning speed. "Dammit, Alaina, sit down."

She glanced down at the hand he'd wrapped around her wrist, then looked back up and arched one brow.

"Please." He eased his grip, but didn't release her, let loose of the breath he'd been holding when she settled back in her seat.

"All right." He pressed his mouth into a hard line. "Maybe I have been a little tense."

"Maybe?" She tilted her head. "A little?"

"Okay," he said through his teeth. "I admit it. I didn't want you coming to town by yourself. You're a beautiful woman, Alaina, and on Saturdays this town is full of horny ranch hands looking for a little fun."

"And you think because I fell into your bed so easy, I'd come to town and—"

"Goddammit, no." Anger flared in his eyes. "I didn't think that."

"I'm sorry," she said quietly, then sighed. "I know you didn't. But, D.J., I work on a ranch, for heaven's sake. I work with men day in and day out. You might not believe it, but I really do know how to block a pass."

"Maybe so." Shaking his head slowly, he brushed his thumb over her hand, and her softness rippled up his arm in a slow river of electricity. "But I don't want them looking at you like that. I don't want them thinking what I know they're thinking."

When Alaina stared at him in stunned silence, he felt like a fool, wanted to kick himself for all but beating his chest. Dammit, what the hell was he thinking? He'd never said anything like that to a woman before, and he had no right to say it now, not when he wasn't offering her anything in return.

But what if he did? He wanted her, he wanted her ranch. What was to say he couldn't have both?

When Stacy suddenly appeared with their drinks, D.J. actually blessed the waitress for her timing, and for continuing her in-depth child rearing discussion with Alaina until their food order was ready. It gave Alaina, and him, time to pretend he hadn't almost complicated their relationship.

They kept their conversation superficial over dinner.

She told him how much she'd enjoyed Bridle Peak and the people, that she'd bought her mother and sisters gifts, a shawl for her mother, some spices for Kiera and a polished rock paperweight for Alexis. She'd also picked up a frame for Dottie that said I Love My Grandma.

It was dark by the time they drove home, and he kept the radio just loud enough to discourage any more talk. He figured he'd said too much already, and what he really wanted wasn't conversation, anyway. The tension of the day had wound him up and the best way to unwind was in his bed, with Alaina naked and underneath him.

With that image in his mind most of the way home, he was already hard by the time he pulled into the driveway at the Rocking B and parked the truck. He came around to open Alaina's door, but she beat him to it, and with her shopping bags in her hands, hurried ahead of him into the house. Frowning, he followed after her, moved up the stairs to find that she'd already gone into her bedroom and closed the door. His frown darkened and he raised a fist to knock, swore instead and went to his own bedroom. He sat on the edge of the bed, tugged his shirt from his jeans, then dragged off one of his boots. He threw it across the room, felt a small bit of satisfaction when it landed against the closet door with a solid thud.

He'd scared her off, dammit. Without meaning to, he'd implied that he wanted an exclusive relationship with her. Considering she was leaving in a week, he didn't know why he'd done that. He dragged off his second boot, started to throw that one, too, then stopped, when a movement in the doorway caught his attention. He turned, stopped breathing when he saw her standing there, wearing a black lace babydoll.

The boot slipped from his hand and dropped to the floor, along with his jaw.

"I bought you something today, too," she said, and moved into the room toward him.

Nine

Alaina had never seduced a man before. Before this morning, she'd never even considered it. She hoped like hell that the shocked look on D.J.'s face and the drop of his jaw meant that she was doing it right.

When his boot had slipped from his fingers and fallen to the floor, she took that as a good sign. In spite of the nerves rattling upward from the tips of her bare toes, she managed to slink toward D.J. without her knees knocking.

"Would you like to unwrap it?" she purred and held out the pencil-box-size package.

"What?" His voice broke, and he swallowed hard.

"Your gift." She took her time closing the distance between them, watched his eyes darken as he took in the plunging V-line of the garment she wore. "Would you like to open it?"

His gaze slid to the satin bow that tied the front of the babydoll together. When he reached for her, she backed away and held out the wrapped box that he obviously hadn't even noticed. It took a moment for his eyes to focus on the package, then he glanced up at her and lifted a brow, clearly debating if he was going for the smaller package, or the bigger one. She held her breath, prepared herself if he made any sudden movements.

But he didn't, just kept his gaze locked with hers and held out his hand until she placed the box in his palm.

He didn't bother to be neat, just tore open the white paper and lifted the lid, then looked inside.

"It's a monocular," she said. "Small enough to fit into a saddlebag. I thought you might like it when you go up to the mesa."

He stared at the gift and his gaze softened for a moment—until he looked back up at her.

"Alaina," he said tightly and set the present aside. "Come here."

The fierce expression in his eyes and the hard set of his jaw made it difficult to breathe. She didn't know what the rules of seduction were, if a true femme fatale would play hard to get or tease a little longer. But her skin was already tingling in anticipation of his touch, her breasts tight and aching for the feel of his hands and mouth. If there *were* rules, she thought, moving closer to him, to hell with them.

She stood in front of him, her heart racing, placed her

palms on his broad shoulders and straddled him. His hands slid down her hips and he cupped her bottom, realized that she wore a thong. His oath could have inspired a gospel. His grip tightened, and the tension shuddered from his body into hers.

Her chest rose and fell rapidly, and the texture of his callused palms on her soft skin sent fire racing through her veins. Slowly she brought her mouth to his and swept her tongue along his bottom lip, took her time tasting and nibbling, until she trembled with need. Wrapping her arms around his neck and her legs around his waist, she deepened the kiss, moaned when he pulled her closer, until his arousal pressed intimately against the V of her thighs. She squirmed against him, wanting him inside her, but black lace and denim kept them apart.

Emotions overwhelmed her, feelings she couldn't tell him, but would show him, instead. Her mind had warned her not to hope for more than this, but her heart hadn't listened. She loved him, and he was part of her now, would always be part of her, no matter what happened.

Her fingers rushed over the buttons of his shirt, then rushed inside to hot, bare skin. His muscles rippled under her fingertips, tightened when she moved her hands lower and unsnapped his jeans. Desire swam through her, clouded her vision, and the urgency, along with the need, grew.

They fell backward onto the bed and her hair tumbled down, spilling over her shoulders onto D.J.'s. She rose over him, felt a power shudder through her unlike anything she'd ever experienced before. *Love,* she thought dimly. Love had made her strong. Made her complete.

She held his gaze, reached for the satin bow at the front of her babydoll, then slowly pulled one end of the ribbon. She stared down at him, watched his dark gaze shift downward to her breasts. When the black lace parted and she splayed her hands low on her stomach, she heard his intake of breath, felt the coiled restraint in his body. He didn't move, just watched her, and the raw, fierce need in his eyes gave her courage. She slid her hands up her belly, her rib cage, lingered on her breasts, then upward, until lace shimmered down her arms and fell away.

He reached for her, and she closed her eyes when his hands covered her breasts and caressed her. She felt as if she were floating on a wave of heat, and when his mouth replaced his hands, she rose higher, where the air was hotter, thinner. She was certain she called his name, heard the distant sound of a moan, hers, his, and then they were tumbling again and he was inside her, where she wanted him, where she needed him.

Pleasure shuddered, dark and wild, then broke, slamming through her again and again as she fell off the edge. Holding tight, she brought him with her.

It was a long time before he could breathe, even longer until he could move. Beside him, Alaina laid motionless, except for the rapid rise and fall of her chest. Somehow he found the strength to reach for her and drag her into his arms.

"Wow," he said hoarsely.

He felt her smile against his shoulder.

Their bodies were slick with sweat, still humming from the intensity of their lovemaking. They were both naked, though with his mind still reeling, it took him a moment to remember exactly how they'd achieved that state. Damn.

He owed her a new thong.

He didn't know what to say. He'd never experienced anything like this before, wasn't even certain he knew what—other than the obvious—had happened. He was completely off balance here, but why should that surprise him. He'd been off balance since the moment he'd met her.

The question was, what was he going to do about it?

When she pressed her lips to his chest, he decided he didn't need an answer right now. "You all right?"

She nipped at his skin. "You tell me."

Chuckling he pulled her closer. "Better than all right, I'd say."

"Good answer." She settled into the crook of his arms, but her fingers, restless and warm, moved in a circle on his chest. "You were better than all right, too."

"That so?"

She gasped when he rolled her underneath him. He kissed her deeply, tenderly, until he could feel her melting again, then lifted his head and gazed down at her. "Thank you."

Her eyes fluttered open. "For what?"

"My present."

A smile curved her kiss-swollen lips. "Which one?"

"Both." He touched her cheek, then traced her mouth with his fingertip. He wanted to tell her what both of her gifts meant to him, but he didn't have the words. "Anytime you want to go shopping again, just let me know."

"I'll do that."

When she pulled his mouth back to hers, he felt the heat flood through his veins again and before he couldn't think at all, wondered how the hell he was going to let this woman go.

Moonlight shimmered over the treetops, sprinkled silver through the tall branches. The scent of jasmine drifted on the cool night, carried with it the sound of a nightingale. Peace settled over the forest, soft as a lover's whisper, smooth as a silken scarf.

She sat beside the fire, warmed her chilled hands over the dancing flames. Contentment vibrated through her fingertips; she belonged here, with the night, with the fire. From the shadows, the Elders watched, and she felt their approval.

Her lover would be here soon, she was certain. She'd never seen his face, but she'd always known he was The One. She'd waited for him a lifetime and excitement raced through her; she longed for his welcoming embrace.

A breeze shuddered through the branches overhead, then rustled the bushes. She heard the crunch of leaves and smiled, then turned, eager to be in her lover's arms.

No one was there.

The air turned icy, and she shivered, then stiffened when the wolf stepped out of the darkness. Barring his teeth, he moved closer, blood dripping from his fangs. Afraid, she shrank back, one hand clutching her throat, the other her heart. Desperately she wanted to run, but fear held her in place, strong and cold as steel shackles.

"No," she cried when the wolf leaned back on its haunches, then sprang. "No!"

"Alaina, easy." D.J. held the arms she'd clutched to her chest. "It's just a dream, baby. Just a bad dream."

She blinked, watched the darkened bedroom come into focus, then remembered where she was. In D.J.'s bedroom, in his bed. *A dream,* she thought, closing her eyes again in relief. *Thank God.*

"You're shaking." He pulled her close, pressed his lips to her forehead. "It's fine, now. I'm here."

"I'm sorry." She buried her head in his shoulder, embarrassed, but moved by the tenderness in his touch. "I didn't mean to wake you."

"I don't mind." Gently he stroked her back. "Wanna talk about it?"

Talk about it? She'd never told anyone her dreams, she realized, good or bad. She heard the beat of his heart against her ear, felt the warmth of his skin, the strength of his muscles. His closeness soothed her frazzled nerves and she relaxed against him.

Maybe if it had just been a dream, a simple nightmare, she could have shared it with him. But it wasn't; she knew in her heart it wasn't, and that frightened her more than the dream.

From the beginning, she'd known that the drums had been a warning. A warning she had foolishly ignored.

"I'm fine now." She didn't want to think about the dreams anymore. This moment, right now, was all that mattered. Pressing her mouth to D.J.'s strong chest, she tasted the salt on his skin, and her own desire. "I don't really feel like talking."

"Okay." D.J.'s heart jumped when she slid her hand down. "So you just want to go back to sleep, then?"

She shook her head while her mouth began to follow the path her hand had taken. "I have all this energy all of a sudden."

"Yeah?" He sucked in a sharp breath. "So what do you want to do?"

Smiling, she kissed the edge of his rib cage, then moved lower. "Why don't I show you?"

Experience had taught Alaina that horses—especially stallions—could be highly unpredictable creatures. No element of training was more important than trust, and until that bond was complete, she knew she had to be on her guard at all times, to never take the animals for granted.

It seemed to her that men weren't so different.

She smiled at the thought, tightened the cinch on Santana's saddle, then gave the horse a friendly pat before she put her boot in the stirrup and swung herself onto the animal's back.

"Easy now." She felt Santana's muscles tense and quiver under her, knew he was anxious to run. "That's my boy."

Gathering the reins, she gave the stallion time to settle down while she glanced around the yard. In the roundpen, one of the hands worked with a bay, and in the corral next to the barn, Bobby exercised a bay gelding. She heard the hum of a tractor behind the barn, a distant radio wailing Brooks and Dunn, the screech of a hawk overhead.

Two days, she thought. Two more days and she'd be gone.

She knew it was a mistake to allow herself to believe they might have a future. But she'd seen something in his eyes the past few days, felt something in his touch, and fool that she was, she'd let herself dream, had dared to hope that he might ask her to stay. It frightened her that he wouldn't ask her almost as much as it frightened her that he would. Because if he did, she would have to tell him the truth about herself.

She'd never told anyone outside her family. Had never wanted to before now. Before D.J.

At the sound of the dogs barking excitedly, she turned and saw him riding in from one of the pastures with Judd and two other hands. As always, her stomach fluttered at the sight of him and her pulse quickened. She watched him, etched his image in her mind, prayed that she would be able to recall every detail. The lines at the corner of his eyes when he frowned, the tight set of his jaw when he was angry, the groves beside his mouth that deepened when he smiled. There were other details, of course, more intimate. The touch of his lips, the taste of his skin, the feel of his hands. She'd locked them all into her mind, into her heart.

When Santana pranced underneath her, Alaina pulled her attention back to the horse. Though he was still a little skittish, the stallion had healed completely, inside and out. She rubbed a hand down his long neck, certain there would be ribbons in his future and lots of wonderful babies. She hoped she'd be able to see them one day.

"What do you say, boy?" With a light press of her knee, she turned the horse toward the trail leading to the river. "Let's go for a ride."

Easing Santana into a canter, Alaina guided him through the stand of trees behind D.J.'s house, decided they could both use a good run. When they moved into an open, flat meadow dotted with Indian Blanket, she let the horse have his head. He shot forward, hooves pounding, dirt flying, and flew across the land, streaked past an oak, circled an outcropping of boulders, then raced toward the river.

Exhilarated, Alaina gave a whoop. She'd ridden hundreds of horses, but none that were more magnificent than this one. She leaned forward in the saddle, ignored the strands of hair that had broken from her braid and whipped across her face. They raced on, the scent of flowering snakeweed heavy in the warm afternoon air, and white, wispy clouds spotting the deep blue sky. A perfect day, she thought, reining the stallion in as they approached the bank of the river. The sun sparkled like diamonds off the rushing water and fat cattle grazed the hillsides, the peacefulness broken only by the distant sound of Taffy's and Baxter's barking, then D.J.'s shrill whistle.

One more moment to cherish and hold close, to always remember.

They ground to a halt at the water's edge, where the river was narrow and shallow, edged with thick shrub and a small grove of cypress. Three days ago, the first time she'd taken Santana out of the corral, D.J. had ridden here with her. They'd sat under the shade of a tree while their horses cropped grass, and he'd told her that his father had brought him fishing here when he was a boy, that sometimes his mother would join them and sit on the bank, a book in her hand and a thermos of iced lemonade at her feet.

Alaina looked down at the riverbank, pictured the woman sitting here, reading her Dick Francis novel, glancing up every so often to smile encouragement at her husband and son. Alaina felt the love that still lingered here, and then the image blurred, and Alaina suddenly saw her own face instead of D.J.'s mother, saw herself watching a grown-up D.J. and a young boy laughing as they reeled in a wiggling, silver fish. His son, she thought.

Their son.

Wishful thinking, she realized. Dangerous thinking.

Cursing her foolishness, she turned Santana toward the shade of the trees. She felt as if she'd always known this place, the ranch, the land. Every tree, every crop of grass, every stone. Her chest ached at the thought of leaving, and she couldn't stop the thickening in her throat, couldn't stop the moisture gathering in her eyes.

Tell him you love him, a tiny voice whispered in her

mind, but she shook her head. She wasn't brave enough, was certain she would die if he couldn't say the words back.

She brushed her tears away, realized the left rein had slipped from her hand. With a sigh, she stood in the stirrups, braced her hand on the saddle horn as she leaned down.

Her fingers were inches away from the rein when Baxter and Taffy burst from the underbrush on the heels of a zigzagging rabbit.

Santana lunged upward, and the stallion's neck slammed into Alaina's shoulder, knocking her from the saddle. Because she knew she couldn't stop herself from falling, instinct took over and she went with it, watched the ground rise up to meet her at the same time Santana kicked out his back hooves, making contact with a sickening, bone-cracking thud.

Not with Alaina, but with Baxter.

The dog yelped as he flew in the air, then dropped with a thud, his body limp and still. Blood, bright red, seeped from his head, and he lay motionless, his eyes closed.

No, please God, no.

"Baxter," she called to the dog as she pushed up on her elbow, ignored the pain that shot through her shoulder and the stars that burst in front of her eyes. She would have grabbed onto Santana's saddle to pull herself up, but the horse had danced nervously several feet away.

Struggling to her feet, Alaina staggered toward the wounded animal, calling to him, prayed he would at least open his eyes, that she could reach him before it was too late. Whimpering, Taffy crawled on her belly toward Baxter, her head low and ears back, her nose twitching with the smell of blood.

"Alaina!"

She heard the sound of D.J.'s voice, the thunder of hooves as he rode up, but she didn't even raise her head. She dropped onto the ground beside Baxter, laid her hands over the animal's chest, felt a fleeting shimmer of life there through the fur and skin.

Don't you die, she thought, splaying her fingers. *Don't you dare die.*

Closing her eyes, she knew she would have to go deep inside herself if she was going to help this animal. She let the calm settle over her, warm and soothing, felt it gather force under her rib cage and pulse and spread through her veins. The vibration increased, and as it always had, took on a life of its own. She did not attempt to control it, knew that she couldn't even if she wanted to. She was simply a conduit for the energy that coursed through her, a channel for a power she'd never asked for or understood.

A heartbeat sounded in her ears, grew stronger, louder. *Baxter's heartbeat.* Her mind filled with an explosion of white, and in the distance, D.J. calling her name. She felt him beside her, touching her, but she kept her eyes closed, didn't move. Dimly she knew she would have to deal with the cost of him witnessing this. But that would be later. Now, she could only stay the course.

When she heard the whimper, she wasn't certain if

it was Taffy or Baxter, but then she felt the movement under her hands, a deep, life-giving breath, then a quiver of flesh. The light dimmed, and her mind slowly cleared. A warm, rough tongue licked at her hand, and then her arms were filled with dog.

Her eyes fluttered open and Baxter greeted her with a wet, sloppy kiss on the cheek. Joy surged through her, made her heart leap. Smiling, she hugged the animal, then felt Taffy nudging in closer to lick Baxter's face.

But her elation was short lived. When she turned to D.J., she saw the disbelief in his shocked gaze. He stared at her without speaking, without moving. She wanted to explain, knew she didn't have much time. But even as she said his name, even as she struggled to find the words, she knew it was too late.

The blackness reached up and grabbed her, squeezed tighter, then tighter still, until it completely closed around her.

She woke slowly to the sound of a steady beep and the scent of antiseptic. A fog had settled over her brain, where a tiny little man with a great big hammer worked furiously to drive nails into her skull. The headache would pass quickly, she knew, as would the roll of nausea. She rode the unpleasant sensations as she would a wave, and when it finally crashed, she opened her eyes.

Where on earth…?

The dimly lit room was empty, void of pictures on the walls. A television hung on the wall, its screen black. She heard the distant sound of a man's voice, a woman answering, then the ring of a bell. Dammit, dammit, *dammit.*

She was in the hospital.

Baxter. It came back to her in a rush, and she bit back the groan deep in her throat, then blinked to clear the last mists of her fog away. She'd passed out before she'd been able to tell D.J. what would happen. That he shouldn't worry, and she would be fine after she slept.

Of course, she doubted he would have believed her, anyway. She would have simply sounded like a crazy woman.

She saw him then, standing by the window, staring out into the night, his shoulders stiff and his jaw tight. How was she ever going to explain? She searched frantically for words, was still searching when he glanced over his shoulder at her. His gaze met hers, hardened and he slowly turned.

"You okay?"

"Yes." Her throat was dry, her voice hoarse. "D.J.—"

"I'll go get the doctor."

"No." She sat, but a little too quickly and the room started to spin. "No, please. Just give me a minute. That's all I need. Just a minute."

She touched her fingertips to her temple, waited a moment for her balance to come back. "How long have I been out?"

"Five hours." He stayed by the window. "I brought you into town straight after—" He stopped, and a muscle twitched when he narrowed his eyes. "I got your sister's number off your cell phone and called her."

Alaina nodded, said a prayer of thanks that he'd called Kiera, not Trey. "What did she tell you?"

"Not enough." He snapped the words out. "Just that I should let you sleep and you'd be fine when you woke up in a few hours."

"I am fine." Even her headache was gone now, she thought, pushing the sheets away. "Where are my clothes?"

"Where are your clothes?" His voice was raspy and tight. He took a step toward her, stopped. "You give me the scare of a lifetime, then ask me where your clothes are?"

"D.J., I'm fine now." But the distance he kept between them frightened her. "Can we just leave now?"

He shook his head. "Not until you tell me what the hell happened out there this afternoon."

"Is Baxter all right?" she asked, wanting to avoid his question almost as much as she wanted to know about the dog.

"That's what I'm talking about, Alaina." He stared at her, a mixture of confusion and disbelief. "Baxter is great, barely a scratch. Santana kicked that dog in the head and threw him fifteen feet. An animal doesn't just get up and dance around after a blow like that."

"Maybe it was just a graze," she said weakly.

"I want to know what you did."

"I don't know how to tell you." She drew in a breath, released it slowly. "How do I explain something I don't understand myself?"

"Try."

She laid back on the bed, stared at the ceiling. "It's just part of me. Who I am. When an animal is hurt, I have to help them, to touch them, and then it just happens."

"It." He narrowed his eyes. "What the hell is *it?*"

"It just is," she whispered. "Like an energy, of sorts, that moves through me, a sensation that transforms and restores balance."

"You're telling me you're a healer?"

She winced at the word as much as the cold glint in his eyes. "If you need to give it a label, then fine." She lifted her chin, met his gaze. "Yes, that's what I am."

He stared at her for a long moment, then turned away and moved to the window again.

"Did you use it on me?"

She had to swallow the thickness in her throat before she could answer. "No, I didn't *use* it on you."

"That first day I met you, when Santana's hoof caught my arm. Something happened then, didn't it?"

"That had never happened to me before, D.J.," she said quietly. "Not with a person. But when I touched you, yes, something happened."

"So you know what I'm thinking, too? What I'm feeling? If I'm going to take a trip or win the lottery?"

"Of course not. I'm not psychic, D.J."

"Santana." He dragged a hand through his hair. "The kitten. Baxter. You—"

"Helped them," she finished for him when he hesitated. "Yes, I did. I can't always help an animal that's hurt, especially if it's too late, but when I can, I do."

"I don't believe it. I saw it, but I don't believe it." Like a caged animal he started to pace. "How have you and your family managed to keep this quiet?"

"We have to." She sighed, thought about how many times she'd had to explain away an animal's incredible recovery. How many animals she hadn't been able to help because someone was watching. "The cloud of scandal we live under because of my father is bad enough. The last thing my family needs is attention like this."

She closed her eyes, rubbed at the nagging throb in her temple. "You think I like being different from other women—hell, from other people? But I didn't choose this, D.J., it chose me. I accept it. I'm sorry I never told you, D.J.," she said quietly. "I should have trusted you."

"No, Alaina—" a deep, familiar voice came from the doorway "—you shouldn't have."

"Trey?" Stunned, Alaina watched her brother move into the room, then glanced at D.J. and narrowed her eyes. "Did you—"

D.J. shook his head.

"Are you all right?" Trey asked tightly.

"Yes, of course, I am." She saw the concern in Trey's eyes, and the controlled anger, prayed he wasn't going to make a scene. "But what are you doing here, how did you—"

"I haven't heard from you for a couple of days, so I called Kiera. It didn't take me long to figure out something was wrong and get the truth out of her."

"Trey—"

"We'll talk about it later," Trey said, then looked at D.J. "You gonna tell her, Bradshaw, or shall I?"

D.J.'s mouth pressed into a hard line. "What the hell are you talking about?"

"Trey, please." The tension in the room was fist tight. She had to stop this before it got out of hand between the two men. "If you'll just let me—"

"I'll tell her then." Trey kept his cold gaze leveled at D.J. "This man you think you should trust didn't just want to buy a horse from us, Alaina. He wants our ranch, too."

Alaina looked at D.J. That was absurd. He'd never said anything to her about buying Stone Ridge Stables. Trey had to be wrong.

"Where did you hear that?" D.J. asked tightly.

"I know a few people," Trey said. "They know a few people. Things leak out. Seems that you've been quietly buying up smaller ranches all over South Texas."

"D.J.?" Breath held, Alaina waited for D.J. to deny it, wondered why he hadn't already. When he didn't, she knew it was true. Dear God, it was true.

What an idiot she was. Hadn't she questioned why a man with D.J.'s money and man power would personally come to Stone ridge Stables to buy a horse? Why he'd want her to come finish Santana's training at his ranch? When she'd asked him not to tell Trey, she'd played right into his hands.

Right into his arms.

The thought ripped through her heart. "Trey, could you give me a moment alone with D.J., please?"

When Trey hesitated, she looked at him, implored him with her eyes. He shot a warning glance at D.J., then turned and left the room.

"All this time," she said quietly, "it was Stone Ridge Stables you wanted."

"I had an offer drawn up to buy your ranch, yes." There was no apology in his voice.

"Did you really think that bringing be to the Rocking B and sleeping with me would influence our decision to sell?"

"Dammit, Alaina," he said through clenched teeth. "One has nothing to do with the other."

The fact that he might actually believe that only ripped the hole in her heart wider. "Strange, but for me, it does. But then, what do I know about these things? I don't get out much."

He swore again, took a step toward her, but she put up a hand to stop him. "I'm going to leave now, with Trey. I'd appreciate it if you'd give me a head start to get back to your ranch and get my things. It will be easier that way, for all of us."

"We're not leaving it like this, Alaina," he said tightly.

"Yes, D.J., I am." She slid out of bed, straightened when her bare feet touched the cool tile floor. "Now if you don't mind, I'd like to get dressed and leave."

A muscle jumped in his jaw, and her heart stopped when she thought he might reach out to her, was certain she'd fall apart if he did.

But the moment passed and he simply turned and walked out. When he knees nearly buckled, she laid a hand on the bed to steady herself. Don't think, she told herself. Don't feel.

She felt the river of ice move through her, welcomed the numbness to the pain she knew would come later.

Ten

There was always work to be done on a ranch and over the next two days, D.J. made it his own personal mission to do it all himself.

Today, he'd left long before the sun had come up, spent his morning in the northeast boundary of the Rocking B checking fence, then headed for the north pasture where he'd looked in on his yearlings. His afternoon had consisted of moving a small herd of cattle to higher ground, then rounding up strays, but one stubborn longhorn had persistently given him grief. After a long, drawn out battle of wills and a stinging rope burn, D.J. had finally emerged the victor.

Not that the stupid cow gave a damn.

He rode in now from the river's bend where he'd

spent the afternoon repairing a jammed windmill pump. Work was the one thing, the only thing that seemed to block out thoughts of Alaina, though more often than not, she crept in anyway, usually at the worst possible time. His distraction had resulted in a bruised ankle, a deep scratch from a line of barbed wire and a lump on his shin the size of a walnut—the outcome of dropping an anvil he'd been moving in the tack room.

He welcomed the physical pain, knew how to deal with it much better than the twist in his gut and the ache in his chest.

He'd told himself he was glad she'd left like she had. No tearful goodbye, no angry accusation. She'd simply left.

And if he'd stayed in town that night and had a few too many beers, so what? She'd wanted to leave without letting him explain, so fine. He'd never explained himself or his business to any woman before and he wasn't about to start now. And if he'd felt a twinge in his chest when he'd driven back into the yard the next morning and seen her truck gone, that didn't mean anything, either, dammit.

He slowed his horse when they reached the outcropping of rocks by the river. He could almost see the tips of cypress from this spot, and once again, for the hundredth time, the image of her kneeling beside Baxter jumped into his head. Her hands on the dog's chest, her eyes closed, her face intent, but peaceful. He thought she'd been hurt, too, and he'd never known that kind of cold fear before. When she passed out, he'd checked her for injuries, but he'd seen nothing. He'd driven her to the hospital like a bat out of hell, had already checked her in before he had the presence of mind to track down her sister.

He'd wanted to yell at Kiera when she'd told him to wait it out, and that Alaina would be fine. How could she be fine? She'd passed out. And after what she'd done—

Oh hell, he just couldn't seem to wrap his brain around it.

She'd left two sealed notes on the kitchen table. One for Dottie, one for Bobby. Nothing for him.

He hadn't lied to her, dammit. So he'd wanted to buy her ranch. That was business, that's all.

Renewed frustration had him urging Sergeant to run again. D.J. managed, just barely, not to think about Alaina until he reached the edge of the ranch, but when Baxter and Taffy came barking up to greet him, there she was again, in Baxter's happy bark and Taffy's goofy gallop.

She was everywhere, and it was making him crazy.

The dogs followed him into the barn and Baxter, noticeably more cautious now, kept a respectable distance from Sergeant's hooves. At least the *dog* had learned something from getting kicked, D.J. thought with a sigh.

D.J. looked around the stalls for Bobby, then slid off his horse. When Alaina had been here, the hand had never been far away. Since she'd been gone, D.J. barely saw the kid.

He started to yell for the hand again, but then he heard singing from Santana's stall, and he froze.

Blue Bayou.

It wasn't Alaina's voice. It was Bobby's, off-key, and most of the words wrong. Furrowing his brow, D.J. stepped to the stall, watched the ranch hand brush the stallion while he quietly sang.

D.J. stood at the open stall door and frowned. Wasn't it bad enough he couldn't get the woman out of his mind? Did he have to hear that damn song, too?

"You singing, or is that horse just stepping on your toe?" D.J. said with more irritation than he intended.

Good-natured kid that he was, Bobby just smiled. "Santana likes it."

"Says who?" D.J. watched Baxter and Taffy stick their noses into the stall and sniff, but he held them back with a command and the dogs sat.

"Alaina." Bobby moved to the horse's hind quarters. "She told me in her note that if Santana got tense or nervous to sing 'Blue Bayou.' Calms him right down every time."

"What makes you think that 'Row, Row, Row Your Boat,' wouldn't work just as well?" D.J. argued, when the question he really wanted to ask was what else Alaina had said in her note.

"I tried a bunch of different ones, but this one's the one." Bobby looked over, a hopeful look in his eyes. "You heard from her?"

D.J. pressed his mouth into a hard line. Bobby was the only hand who didn't have the sense not to ask a question like that. "Go see to Sergeant," he snapped and moved into the stall. "I'll finish here."

"Sure, boss." Somewhat reluctantly, Bobby handed

him the brush, then shoved his hands into his front pockets. "So if you do talk to her, will you tell her I said hi?"

"Sure," D.J. said through gritted teeth, waited for the hand to leave before he swore, then muttered under his breath, "She's gone. Deal with it."

When Santana snorted, D.J. frowned, noticed that Baxter and Taffy were still sitting at the stall door, intently watching him. "Stop looking at me like I'm the bad guy here, all of you. I didn't ask her to leave—it was her decision."

When the dogs lowered their heads and Santana stomped a hoof, D.J. swore again. "I didn't ask her to leave, dammit. I didn't *want* her to leave!"

His hand tightened on the brush and he felt three pairs of eyes boring into him. He could hear the question inside his head as loudly as if he'd shouted it with a bullhorn.

So why did you let her?

"Alaina, for heaven's sake, we're taking you to have dinner, not a root canal. Will you please relax?"

Sitting in the back seat of the hotel Town Car, Alaina stared out at the passing landscape and prayed she wouldn't lose what little lunch she'd had earlier at the Four Winds. "I am relaxed."

"Right." Rolling her eyes, Kiera glanced over her shoulder from the front seat. "That's why you've got a death grip on the armrest."

Alaina shot her sister a cool look, then turned her attention to the man driving the car. "Sam, will you please tell your fiancée that she should be more respectful of her elders, and that I'd appreciate a little quiet time before I meet the people whose lives our father nearly destroyed."

"Be happy to." Grinning, Sam looked at his bride-to-be. "Your sister says—"

"Never mind." Kiera sighed and turned around, folding her arms. "You've got about ten minutes before we get there. I'll zip it until then."

In spite of her nerves and the knots twisting her stomach, Alaina couldn't help but smile. Kiera had been clucking over her like a mother hen for the past three days, cooking her special meals in the hotel suite that Sam had reserved for her, bringing her flowers from the hotel florist, handing her tissues to dry her eyes and blow her nose.

It was humiliating, crying over a man.

Amazingly, she'd managed to convince Trey not to follow her to Wolf River and she'd been grateful she'd had the time alone to pull herself together on the four hour drive.

She'd finally walked into the Four Winds, had greatly appreciated that Kiera hadn't questioned her middle of the night arrival, she'd simply hugged her, then led her to her room and insisted she sleep. Not one question had been asked about D.J., or what had happened.

She stared blankly down at the deep, dry river creek that ran along the two lane road. The land was rocky here, with oak trees and coyote bush, pretty in its isolation, craggy hills, and spots of pink wildflowers. It was the first time in three days she'd been outside the hotel.

It had taken her that long to find her balance again, to finally put her feet on the ground and stand straight. The past two days she hadn't been so sure, but today she knew that she'd be a little stronger every day, and that slowly, day by day, the pain would ease. D.J. had lied to her, even used her and even though her heart might be broken, she'd have her life back, and eventually she'd even find joy again. In her work, with her family.

With another man.

She closed her eyes at the thought, let the pain ripple through her, and willed herself to believe that. She had to believe it. How else could she move on?

She heard the crunch of gravel under the tires and the bark of a dog, looked up and saw Rand and Grace Blackhawk's brand new one story ranch house. It was a beautiful Cape Cod blue with white trim, lots of windows and gabled roof lines. A riot of yellow and white daisies spilled from flower beds and pots on the wide, brick entry.

"Are you sure I'm dressed all right?" Alaina glanced down at her jeans and blue blouse, had wanted to wear something nicer, but Kiera had insisted they were all going for a ride to see Rand's ranch, and riding clothes were a requirement.

"You look great." Kiera smiled, then tilted her head. "You ready?"

Biting her lip, Alaina nodded.

Sam parked the car in front of a three-car garage, then stepped out and opened the door for her. She took the hand he offered and managed a smile, even though her heart was pumping like a steel bellow.

She hardly knew her sister's fiancé, but she'd liked him the moment she'd met him. Not just the tall, handsome exterior, but the inner man, as well. He was good for Kiera—perfect, she thought. It was obvious he loved her, and she loved him. As happy as that made her, she still couldn't stop the twist of pain in her chest for the love she'd lost.

"They won't bite." Kiera slipped her arm through Alaina's. "I promise you'll love them."

When the front door opened, Alaina's eyes widened. Kiera had told her how much Rand Blackhawk looked like Trey, and it was true. Before she could hold her hand out, Rand had wrapped his big arms around her and hugged.

There were more hugs from other cousins. Lucas, Seth, Dillon. Even Clair, who'd been battling morning sickness in her second month of pregnancy, had shown up for the casual family gathering. The wives all hugged her next and she tried to keep the names and couples straight: Grace with Rand; Julianna with Lucas; Jacob with Clair; Hannah with Seth. Dillon with Rebecca. And the children! There were so many of the little munchkins, all of them except the babies currently chasing several large balls around the backyard. Alaina knew it would take her some time to get to know who went with whom, but time was the one thing she had.

There was love here, Alaina thought as she stood in the middle of everyone talking at once and the children running in and out with a golden retriever pup jumping at their heels. She could see the love. Could feel it.

And strangely, it felt like home.

Alaina wished that Trey were here, that he could be a part of this. She knew it would be hard for him to let these people into his life, to trust them. Trey had been the one to keep their family together after their father had abandoned them and their mother had drifted into another reality. Growing up, they'd only had each other and that had been all they needed. But they were grown now, lives of their own. It was a difficult concept for Trey, but in time, he'd come to accept it.

"Kiera tells me you've been at the Rocking B," Rand said, handing Alaina an iced tea after they'd all moved into the backyard and broken into smaller groups.

Even though she'd known that sooner or later D.J.'s name would come up, even though she'd told herself she wouldn't blink when it did, she still stiffened. "I was working with a stallion D.J. bought from our stables."

"Santana." Rand took a pull on the bottle of beer in his hands. "Kiera mentioned the horse to me. Sounds like D.J. got a great animal."

"He's a champion." She couldn't help the pride that swelled in her, or the ache. "Kiera tells me you're just getting your ranch started up again. You might want to look at some of our stock."

"I'll do that," Rand said with a nod, then glanced at Kiera. "There's something Kiera and I would like to talk to you about, privately."

Alaina stiffened, glanced at Kiera, who was standing with Sam and Lucas. Her sister never would have told Rand about her relationship with D.J., especially considering the two men were good friends. But when Kiera suddenly looked over, then excused herself from her conversation, and moved across the lawn, Alaina suddenly wasn't so certain. "Oh?"

"Why don't we step inside?" Rand suggested, and moved to a pair of French doors off the patio that led into an airy office with built in desks and shelves. When Kiera joined them and Rand closed the doors, Alaina felt her pulse quicken.

She stood there, her fingers tightening on the glass in her hand, glanced from Kiera to Rand, but couldn't read their expressions. Why were they both staring at her so strangely? Alaina swore she'd seriously hurt her sister if she'd even mentioned—

"You should probably give me that glass and sit down," Kiera said, reaching for the tea.

"What's wrong?" Alaina furrowed her brow, but because her knees were starting to weaken, she did as Kiera asked.

"Nothing at all." Kiera smiled and looked at Rand. "You tell her. Just give her the short version for now."

Somebody tell me, for God's sake, Alaina wanted to scream.

"Your grandfather left you five million dollars."

Alaina stared at Rand, certain she hadn't heard him right. "What?"

"He knew about your mother," Rand said quietly. "About all of you. Before he died, he left trust funds, with instructions for each of you to be contacted when you turned twenty-five and the money released. When your father found out, he managed to gain control of the funds and transferred them to an offshore account. Two weeks ago, Dillon found the original documents in a safe-deposit box and just three days ago gained possession of the accounts."

Alaina opened her mouth, but no sound came out. She looked at Kiera, who knelt beside her and grinned.

"Five million dollars in a trust bearing account for twenty-five years," Kiera said, and there was disbelief in her eyes, too. "Sister, that's a lot of money."

She couldn't even fathom how much. Alaina blinked several times. This wasn't real. It couldn't be.

"It took me a couple of days to absorb it," Kiera said softly. "I wanted you to be here, with everyone, when we told you."

She lifted a shaky hand to her temple. "Does Alexis know? And Trey?"

"I thought we'd tell them together, in person." Kiera squeezed Alaina's fingers. "It'll be more fun, don't you think?"

Good Lord, she didn't know what to think. All that money? She couldn't stop shaking her head. "What will we do with it all?"

"Oh, we'll think of something," Kiera said, laughing. "Let's go for a ride, sis. Just you and me. Talk about it."

"But everyone is here," Alaina protested. "We can't just—"

"I've got two horses saddled for you." Grinning, Rand pulled Alaina to her feet. "Think you can manage to stay in the saddle?"

"I—I think so."

Kiera grabbed Alaina's hand, dragged her across the lawn while the rest of the family looked on, laughing and smiling. Numb, Alaina stumbled behind her sister. When they reached the barn, Kiera jumped onto the saddle of a pretty calico mare tied to a post, and Alaina swung up on a buckskin gelding. She hadn't ridden with her sister for a long time and Alaina let her lead, galloped after her down a shrub lined dirt trail, then through a meadow dotted with oak trees.

She tried to process the enormity of the money, and what it meant, but strangely, it didn't mean nearly as much as she thought it should. If it did, why would she be thinking about D.J., why would the hole in her heart feel just as deep and empty as it had before? There were things she could do with the money, things she could buy, but nothing came to her mind that she wanted.

Nothing except D.J.

"I'll race you to that tree over there," Kiera yelled over her shoulder, pointing to a large oak on the other side of the meadow.

Maybe this would ease some of the heartache, Alaina thought, and let her horse have its head. She raced past her sister, felt the wind whip her hair and stream over her face. When she got back to Stone Ridge, she would start working with that palomino yearling they'd picked up at auction, then there was Reinhold's Light, the two-year-old bay who hadn't learned his manners yet. She also had a fall garden to plant and she'd been trying to learn to knit, though the one scarf she made looked more like a stretched out dishrag.

In time, work would heal her. And Kiera's upcoming wedding, she thought. It hurt, and she knew it would for a long time.

I'm not my mother, she told herself firmly. She'd survive without D.J. She'd always love him, but she'd survive.

Glancing over her shoulder, she saw that Kiera had fallen way behind. Culinary school and all that cooking had turned her little sister into a tenderfoot. Smiling, she turned back and when she looked at the oak tree, her smile faded.

A lone rider sat under the shade of the wide branches.

Heart pounding, she reined her horse in, had to blink to make sure she wasn't hallucinating.

D.J. And Santana. Just sitting under that oak tree as if it were the most natural thing in the world.

Alaina looked back at her sister, saw that she'd ridden back in the direction of the house. *The little sneak.*

She'd deal with Kiera later, she told herself and eased her horse back into a walk, gauged the halfway mark between her and D.J. and stopped. Her pulse was racing so hard and fast, she could barely hear over the roar in her ears.

He moved toward her, but his face was shaded under his black Stetson. It took every ounce of strength she possessed to keep herself from jumping off her horse and running to him.

Though it was only seconds, it felt like hours before he finally reached her, before she could see his face.

He looked tired, she thought, and decided that was a good thing.

"Hello, D.J."

"Hello, Alaina."

She felt his gaze on her, intense and longing, and it sucked what little breath she had right out of her lungs. "What are you doing here?"

"Just taking a ride."

"That's one hell of a long ride."

"You have no idea." He slid off Santana, patted the horse's neck. "Santana missed you."

"Is that so?" Alaina's fingers tightened on the reins.

D.J. nodded, came to her side and glanced up at her. "I missed you."

She said nothing, just watched him, her breath held. Whatever it was he'd come here to say, she wouldn't make it easy for him.

"We want you to come back," D.J. said, lacing his fingers with hers. The smile faded from his lips as he met her gaze. "I want you to come back."

His touch weakened her, and she struggled against the need and want threatening to make a fool out of her for a second time. "You lied to me."

A muscle twitched in his hard jaw and he looked away for a long moment, swallowed hard, then looked back. "I'm sorry. I should have told you I was making an offer to buy your ranch. The truth is, I was afraid you'd leave if I did."

His apology and admission surprised her. But it wasn't enough. It simply wasn't enough. "I can't come back," she whispered. "No more than I can change who I am."

In his entire life, nothing had ever scared D.J. as much as the resolve shining in Alaina's blue eyes. If he'd lost her, really lost her, then he'd lost everything.

"I don't want you to change, baby. Not one tiny bit. I want you exactly the way you are." He tightened his hand on hers, afraid to let go. "I *love* you exactly the way you are."

Her eyes widened and she stared down at him, her lips parted in shock. "You—you love me?"

He reached up, wrapped his arms around her waist, dragged her off her horse and pulled her against him. "I've spent a lifetime being alone, found every excuse I could to keep it that way, nice and safe. But then you came along, shooting sparks and electricity, and I ran out of excuses. I fell in love with you the moment I laid eyes on you."

She felt good in his arms, soft and warm and the touch of her hands on his chest gave him strength. "This thing of yours, sweetheart, whatever it is, I love that, too. It's good and pure and I figure you have it for a reason, so who the hell am I to question that? God, please forgive me for being an idiot and tell me you'll come back."

Alaina felt herself weaken, was still reeling with the shock, and the joy, of his admission. She wanted to say yes, that she'd come to him on any terms, but she couldn't.

She touched his face with her fingertips, pressed her lips softly to his and sighed. "I can't come back, D.J.," she whispered. "I saw what that did to my mother, to my family—"

"Stop. Stop right there." D.J.'s eyes narrowed fiercely. "Is that what you think? That I'm asking you to live with me?"

She suddenly felt foolish, didn't know what to think. He'd told her he'd loved her. Asked her to come back—

"Alaina—" he gripped her arms tighter when she tried to pull away "—I'm not asking you to live with me. I'm asking you to marry me."

"You want me to marry you?" she repeated, prayed that she'd heard him right.

She stumbled back when he released her, watched as he reached into the front pocket of his shirt and pulled out a gold band with a simple, but elegant diamond. "This was my mother's," he said quietly, holding the ring out to her. "Will you wear it, at least until I can buy you something bigger?"

Stunned, she stared at the ring, felt the tears burn her eyes and thicken her throat. She wanted to tell him she didn't want anything bigger, that all she wanted was him, but she couldn't find her voice.

"Marry me." He looked into her eyes. "Love me. Have my children."

Marriage. Children. D.J. Everything she'd ever wanted and more. She pressed a hand to her heart, was certain it would beat right out of her chest. "I do love you," she whispered, then jumped into his arms with a laugh. "I do. Yes. Yes."

He swung her, then pulled her close and kissed her, a long, deep kiss that poured his love into her. Joy swelled in her heart. She heard the birds chattering in the oak tree, the call of a hawk overhead, felt the breeze shimmer over her skin. When he set her back down, she held on, afraid her knees wouldn't hold her.

"I love you." He kissed her again and reached for her hand. When their fingers touched, sparks crackled in the dry air. Breath held, she watched him lift his gaze to hers and smile, then slip the ring onto her finger.

"It's beautiful." She stepped back from her, watched the sun sparkle off the diamond. "It's perfect."

A sudden nudge from behind pushed her into D.J.'s arms again. She turned and looked at Santana, then broke into laughter.

"Shall we go back to the house?" D.J. asked after another long, deep kiss.

"Not yet." She rubbed her lips over his, felt the vibrations move from her body into his, then back again. She'd never felt more whole, more loved. She glanced up, realized she hadn't told him about the trust fund, but when he brought his mouth back to her, she knew it didn't matter. They had time to talk later, she thought, kissing him back and smiling.

A lifetime.

* * * * *

Watch for more Blackhawk stories when Barbara McCauley's SECRETS! *Series continues April 2007, only in Silhouette Desire.*

Ambience is everything. Imagine eating a foie gras at a luncheonette counter or a side of coleslaw at Le Cirque. It's not a matter of food but one of atmosphere. Remember that when planning your dining room design.

—Tips from *Teddi.com*

"Now that's the kind of man you should be looking for," my mother, the self-appointed keeper of my shelf-life stamp, says. She points with her fork at a man in the corner of the Steak-Out Restaurant, a dive I've just been hired to redecorate. Making this restaurant look four-star will be hard, but not half as hard as getting through lunch without strangling the woman across the table from me. "*He* would make a good husband."

"Oh, you can tell that from across the room?" I ask, wondering how it is she can forget that when we had trouble getting rid of my last husband, she shot him. "Besides being ten minutes away from death if he actually eats all that steak, he's twenty years too old for me and—shallow woman that I am—twenty pounds too heavy. Besides, I am *so* not looking for another husband here. I'm looking to design a new image for this place, looking for some sense of ambience, some feeling, something I can build a proposal on for them."

My mother studies the man in the corner, tilting her head, the better to gauge his age, I suppose. I think she's grimacing, but with all the Botox and Restylane injected into that face, it's hard to tell. She takes another bite of her steak salad, chews slowly so that I don't miss the fact that the steak is a poor cut and tougher than it should be. "You're concentrating on the wrong kind of proposal," she says finally. "Just look at this place, Teddi. It's a dive. There are hardly any other diners. What does *that* tell you about the food?"

"That they cater to a dinner crowd and it's lunchtime," I tell her.

I don't know what I was thinking bringing her here with me. I suppose I thought it would be better than eating alone. There really are days when my common sense goes on vacation. Clearly, this is one of them. I mean, really, did I not resolve less than three weeks ago that I would not let my mother get to me anymore?

What good are New Year's resolutions, anyway?

Mario approaches the man's table and my mother studies him while they converse. Eventually Mario leaves the table with a huff, after which the diner glances up and meets my mother's gaze. I think she's smiling at him. That or she's got indigestion. They size each other up.

I concentrate on making sketches in my notebook and try to ignore the fact that my mother is flirting. At nearly seventy, she's developed an unhealthy interest in members of the opposite sex to whom she isn't married.

According to my father, who has broken the TMI rule and given me Too Much Information, she has no interest in sex with him. Better, I suppose, to be clued in on what they aren't doing in the bedroom than have to hear what they might be doing.

"He's not so old," my mother says, noticing that I have barely touched the Chinese chicken salad she warned me not to get. "He's got about as many years on you as you have on your little cop friend."

She does this to make me crazy. I know it, but it works all the same. "Drew Scoones is not my little 'friend.' He's a detective with whom I—"

"Screwed around," my mother says. I must look shocked, because my mother laughs at me and asks if I think she doesn't know the "lingo."

What I thought she didn't know was that Drew and I actually tangled in the sheets. And, since it's possible she's just fishing, I sidestep the issue and tell her that Drew is just a couple of years younger than me and that I don't need reminding. I dig into my salad with renewed vigor, determined to show my mother that Chinese chicken salad in a steak place was not the stupid choice it's proving to be.

After a few more minutes of my picking at the wilted leaves on my plate, the man my mother has me nearly engaged to pays his bill and heads past us toward the back of the restaurant. I watch my mother take in his shoes, his suit and the diamond pinkie ring that seems to be cutting off the circulation in his little finger.

"Such nice hands," she says after the man is out of sight. "Manicured." She and I both stare at my hands. I have two popped acrylics that are being held on at weird angles by bandages. My cuticles are ragged and there's marker decorating my right hand from measuring care-lessly when I did a drawing for a customer.

Twenty minutes later she's disappointed that he managed to leave the restaurant without our noticing. He will join the list of the ones I let get away. I will hear about him twenty years from now when—accord-ing to my mother—my children will be grown and I will still be single, living pathetically alone with several dogs and cats.

After my ex, that sounds good to me.

The waitress tells us that our meal has been taken care of by the management and, after thanking Mario, the owner, complimenting him on the wonderful meal and assuring him that once I have redecorated his place people will be flocking here in droves (I actually use those words and ignore my mother when she rolls her eyes), my mother and I head for the restroom.

My father—unfortunately not with us today—has the patience of a saint. He got it over the years of living with my mother. She, perhaps as a result, figures he has the patience for both of them, and feels justified having none. For her, no rules apply, and a little thing like a picture of a man on the door to a public restroom is certainly no barrier to using the john. In all fairness, it does seem silly to stand and wait for the ladies' room if no one is using the men's room.

Still, it's the idea that rules don't apply to her, signs don't apply to her, conventions don't apply to her. She knocks on the door to the men's room. When no one answers she gestures to me to go in ahead. I tell her that I can certainly wait for the ladies' room to be free and she shrugs and goes in herself.

Not a minute later there is a bloodcurdling scream from behind the men's room door.

"Mom!" I yell. "Are you all right?"

Mario comes running over, the waitress on his heels. Two customers head our way while my mother continues to scream.

I try the door, but it is locked. I yell for her to open it and she fumbles with the knob. When she finally manages to unlock and open it, she is white behind her two streaks of blush, but she is on her feet and appears shaken but not stirred.

"What happened?" I ask her. So do Mario and the

waitress and the few customers who have migrated to the back of the place.

She points toward the bathroom and I go in, thinking it serves her right for using the men's room. But I see nothing amiss.

She gestures toward the stall, and, like any self-respecting and suspicious woman, I poke the door open with one finger, expecting the worst.

What I find is worse than the worst.

The husband my mother picked out for me is sitting on the toilet. His pants are puddled around his ankles, his hands are hanging at his sides. Pinned to his chest is some sort of Health Department certificate.

Oh, and there is a large, round, bloodless bullet hole between his eyes.

Four Nassau County police officers are securing the area, waiting for the detectives and crime scene personnel to show up. They are trying, though not very hard, to comfort my mother, who in another era would be considered to be suffering from the vapors. Less tactful in the twenty-first century, I'd say she was losing it. That is, if I didn't know her better, know she was milking it for everything it was worth.

My mother loves attention. As it begins to flag, she swoons and claims to feel faint. Despite four No Smoking signs, my mother insists it's all right for her to light up because, after all, she's in shock. Not to mention that signs, as we know, don't apply to her.

When asked not to smoke, she collapses mournfully

in a chair and lets her head loll to the side, all without mussing her hair.

Eventually, the detectives show up to find the four patrolmen all circled around her, debating whether to administer CPR, smelling salts or simply call the paramedics. I, however, know just what will snap her to attention.

"Detective Scoones," I say loudly. My mother parts the sea of cops.

"We have to stop meeting like this," he says lightly to me, but I can feel him checking me over with his eyes, making sure I'm all right while pretending not to care.

"What have you got in those pants?" my mother asks him, coming to her feet and staring at his crotch accusingly. "*Baydar?* Everywhere we Bayers are, you turn up. You don't expect me to buy that this is a coincidence, I hope."

Drew tells my mother that it's nice to see her, too, and asks if it's his fault that her daughter seems to attract disasters.

Charming to be made to feel like the bearer of a plague.

He asks how I am.

"Just peachy," I tell him. "I seem to be making a habit of finding dead bodies, my mother is driving me crazy and the catering hall I booked two freakin' years ago for Dana's bat mitzvah has just been shut down by the Board of Health!"

"Glad to see your luck's finally changing," he says, giving me a quick squeeze around the shoulders before turning his attention to the patrolmen, asking what they've got, whether they've taken any statements, moved anything, all the sort of stuff you see on TV, without any of the drama. That is, if you don't count my mother's threats to faint every few minutes when she senses no one's paying attention to her.

Mario tells his waitstaff to bring everyone espresso, which I decline because I'm wired enough. Drew pulls him aside and a minute later I'm handed a cup of coffee that smells divinely of Kahlúa.

The man knows me well. Too well.

His partner, whom I've met once or twice, says he'll interview the kitchen staff. Drew asks Mario if he minds if he takes statements from the patrons first and gets to him and the waitstaff afterward.

"No, no," Mario tells him. "Do the patrons first." Drew raises his eyebrow at me like he wants to know if I get the double entendre. I try to look bored.

"What is it with you and murder victims?" he asks me when we sit down at a table in the corner.

I search them out so that I can see you again, I almost say, but I'm afraid it will sound desperate instead of sarcastic.

My mother, lighting up and daring him with a look to tell her not to, reminds him that *she* was the one to find the body.

Drew asks what happened *this time*. My mother tells him how the man in the john was "taken" with me, couldn't take his eyes off me and blatantly flirted with both of us. To his credit, Drew doesn't laugh, but his smirk is undeniable to the trained eye. And I've had my eye trained on him for nearly a year now.

"While he was noticing you," he asks me, "did *you*

notice anything about him? Was he waiting for anyone? Watching for anything?"

I tell him that he didn't appear to be waiting or watching. That he made no phone calls, was fairly intent on eating and did, indeed, flirt with my mother. This last bit Drew takes with a grain of salt, which was the way it was intended.

"And he had a short conversation with Mario," I tell him. "I think he might have been unhappy with the food, though he didn't send it back."

Drew asks what makes me think he was dissatisfied, and I tell him that the discussion seemed acrimonious and that Mario looked distressed when he left the table. Drew makes a note and says he'll look into it and asks about anyone else in the restaurant. Did I see anyone who didn't seem to belong, anyone who was watching the victim, anyone looking suspicious?

"Besides my mother?" I ask him, and Mom huffs and blows her cigarette smoke in my direction.

I tell him that there were several deliveries, the kitchen staff going in and out the back door to grab a smoke. He stops me and asks what I was doing checking out the back door of the restaurant.

Proudly—because, while he was off forgetting me, dropping by only once in a while to say hi to Jesse, my son, or drop something by for one of my daughters that he thought they might like, I was getting on with my life—I tell him that I'm decorating the place.

He looks genuinely impressed. "Commercial customers? That's great," he says. Okay, that's what he

ought to say. What he actually says is "Whatever pays
the bills."

"Howard Rosen, the famous restaurant critic, got her
the job," my mother says. "You met him—the good-
looking, distinguished gentleman with the *real* job,
something to be proud of. I guess you've never read his
reviews in *Newsday.*"

Drew, without missing a beat, tells her that Howard's
reviews are on the top of his list, as soon as he learns
how to read.

"I only meant—" my mother starts, but both of us
assure her that we know just what she meant.

"So," Drew says. "Deliveries?"

I tell him that Mario would know better than I, but
that I saw vegetables come in, maybe fish and linens.

"This is the second restaurant job Howard's got her,"
my mother tells Drew.

"At least she's getting *something* out of the relationship," he says.

"If he were here," my mother says, ignoring the in-
sinuation, "he'd be comforting her instead of interrogat-
ing her. He'd be making sure we're both all right after
such an ordeal."

"I'm sure he would," Drew agrees, then looks me in
the eyes as if he's measuring my tolerance for shock.
Quietly he adds, "But then maybe he doesn't know just
what strong stuff your daughter's made of."

It's the closest thing to a tender moment I can expect
from Drew Scoones. My mother breaks the spell. "She
gets that from me," she says.

Both Drew and I take a minute, probably to pray that's all I inherited from her.

"I'm just trying to save you some time and effort," my mother tells him. "My money's on Howard."

Drew withers her with a look and mutters something that sounds suspiciously like "fool's gold." Then he excuses himself to go back to work.

I catch his sleeve and ask if it's all right for us to leave. He says sure, he knows where we live. I say goodbye to Mario. I assure him that I will have some sketches for him in a few days, all the while hoping that this murder doesn't cancel his redecorating plans. I need the money desperately, the alternative being borrowing from my parents and being strangled by the strings.

My mother is strangely quiet all the way to her house. She doesn't tell me what a loser Drew Scoones is—despite his good looks—and how I was obviously drooling over him. She doesn't ask me where Howard is taking me tonight or warn me not to tell my father about what happened because he will worry about us both and no doubt insist we see our respective psychiatrists.

She fidgets nervously, opening and closing her purse over and over again.

"You okay?" I ask her. After all, she's just found a dead man on the toilet, and tough as she is that's got to be upsetting.

When she doesn't answer me I pull over to the side of the road.

"Mom?" She refuses to meet my eyes. "You want me to take you to see Dr. Cohen?"

She looks out the window as if she's just realized we're on Broadway in Woodmere. "Aren't we near Marvin's Jewelers?" she asks, pulling something out of her purse.

"What have you got, Mother?" I ask, prying open her fingers to find the murdered man's ring.

"It was on the sink," she says in answer to my dropped jaw. "I was going to get his name and address and have you return it to him so that he could ask you out. I thought it was a sign that the two of you were meant to be together."

"He's dead, Mom. You understand that, right?" I ask. You never can tell when my mother is fine and when she's in la-la land.

"Well, I didn't know that," she shouts at me. "Not at the time."

I ask why she didn't give it to Drew, realize that she wouldn't give Drew the time in a clock shop and add, "…or one of the other policemen?"

"For heaven's sake," she tells me. "The man is dead, Teddi, and I took his ring. How would that look?"

Before I can tell her it looks just the way it is, she pulls out a cigarette and threatens to light it.

"I mean, really," she says, shaking her head like it's my brains that are loose. "What does he need with it now?"

Silhouette

SPECIAL EDITION™

Logan's Legacy Revisited

**THE LOGAN FAMILY IS BACK
WITH SIX NEW STORIES.**

Beginning in January 2007 with

THE COUPLE MOST LIKELY TO

by

LILIAN DARCY

Tragedy drove them apart. Reunited eighteen years later, their attraction was once again undeniable. But had time away changed Jake Logan enough to let him face his fears and commit to the woman he once loved?

REQUEST YOUR FREE BOOKS!

2 FREE NOVELS
PLUS 2
FREE GIFTS!

Passionate, Powerful, Provocative!

In February, expect **MORE**
from

HARLEQUIN® *Romance®*

as it increases to six titles per month.

What's to come...

Rancher and Protector

Part of the

Western Weddings
miniseries

BY JUDY CHRISTENBERRY

The Boss's
Pregnancy Proposal

BY RAYE MORGAN

Don't miss February's
incredible line up of authors!

Silhouette

nocturne™

**WAS HE HER SAVIOR
OR HER NIGHTMARE?**

HAUNTED
LISA CHILDS

Years ago, Ariel and her sisters were separated for
their own protection. Now the man who vowed
revenge on her family has resumed the hunt, and
Ariel must warn her sisters before it's too late.
The closer she comes to finding them, the more
secretive her fiancé becomes. Can she trust the man
she plans to spend eternity with? Or has he been
waiting for the perfect moment to destroy her?

On sale December 2006.

Don't miss
DAKOTA FORTUNES,
a six-book continuing series following
the Fortune family of South Dakota—
oil is in their blood and privilege
is their birthright.

This series kicks off with
USA TODAY bestselling author
PEGGY MORELAND'S
Merger of Fortunes
(SD #1771)
this January.

Other books in the series:

BACK IN FORTUNE'S BED by Bronwyn James (Feb)
FORTUNE'S VENGEFUL GROOM by Charlene Sands (March)
MISTRESS OF FORTUNE by Kathie DeNosky (April)
EXPECTING A FORTUNE by Jan Colley (May)
FORTUNE'S FORBIDDEN WOMAN by Heidi Betts (June)
